# TAKEN BY THE ALPHA

KNOTTED OMEGA 1

LAXMI HARIHARAN
SCARLETTE BROOKE

# 1

*CLAIM* your *FREE* prequel of *Wanted by the Alpha, here*

## Zeus

"Boo!" I bare my teeth.

The soldier cringes, and sweat beads his forehead.

"Really, Z?" My second-in-command narrows his gaze.

I raise my shoulders then let them drop. "Okay, a bit over the top." But, cut me some slack, okay? I like to play with my prey.

Besides, I have a flair for the dramatic, one of the few redeeming features I inherited from my bastard of a father. Except, oh, wait, I was the bastard in that relationship, given he'd never acknowledged me...not until I had my fingers around Golan's neck and recognition had dawned in his eyes. Too late, Pater. Thirty years too late.

The soldier's skin is stretched so tight over his cheekbones that I expect it to crack any moment. The reek of piss stinks up the warehouse. The fool, clearly a beta by the way his shoulders are hunched, has wet himself.

I yawn aloud. The sound of my jaws cracking seems to snap the man into action, for he staggers forward, followed by his partner. They haul a rolled-up carpet between them.

Strings of thread trail from the edges to sweep over the wooden floor. The patchwork on the outside of the carpet is peeling. The fabric seems so innocuous, so unassuming, it's precisely that which sends all of my instincts on alert.

A sliver of awareness ripples over my skin. Thud, thud, thud, my heart-beat accelerates. The fine hair on my neck rises.

What the bloody hell? I can't take my gaze off that damn rug. "Unfurl it."

The edge of impatience in my tone must have signaled the impending flare of temper, for Ethan, my second moves forward—not that the soldiers will dare try anything. The stripes on their vests mark them out as emis-saries of the Leader of Scotland, and Kayden doesn't have the balls to put them up to breaking into my stronghold. I drum my fingers over my chest. Nah! It's exactly the kind of move, I'd expect that twat to try to pull off.

Adrenaline laces my blood. I curl my fingers into fists.

That piece of shit wants me out of the way so he can take over my posi-tion. Well, he and most of those gathered here. Don't everyone rush all at once. I snicker.

The Scot nearest to me pales.

He expects me to kill him. The body count I've left behind in the past year ensures that most fear me. But I might spare these men; for now, and only because it keeps them guessing about when they are going to die. Can't have them getting too comfortable now, eh?

I lean forward on the balls of my feet.

The sudden movement draws a gasp from the beta. He bends and places his side of the rolled-up cloth on the floor. The other man follows.

I take a step forward. Honestly, I don't show any other outward sign of threat. I don't even peel back my lips, or speak…well, okay, I glare at the soldier on the right.

With an audible gulp, he turns and scampers down the big hall toward the still open doors. His partner blinks then scoots after him. My gaze is already on the piece of fabric left behind.

"I don't think it's wise to open it, General," Ethan warns.

Since climate change unleashed tsunamis and wrecked Earth's

sublayers thirty years ago, trace metals all but vanished. Electronics can no longer be powered up, and technology collapsed, leaving no means of communicating. The only way to check what's inside that rug is the old-fashioned way. To open it.

"Consider yourself heard." I crack my neck from side to side. "You've done your duty, Second, so can we get this charade over with?"

Sure, his concern is genuine, and yet it doesn't sit easily with me.

Not since he betrayed the ex-General, aka my dear departed father, by aiding me in killing the old man.

"Allow me, sir." Solomon, my third, grabs the open seam of the curled-up mat. He heaves, but it doesn't budge.

Ethan moves to the other side, and together they tug at it. The cloth unfurls…and flattens out into a pool of turquoise and green.

The illumination from the solitary skylight far above floods over it and the entire rug shimmers.

My pulse races. The breath catches in my throat. My heart hammers and I am sure it's going to jump out of my ribcage.

The next second, a figure springs up from the carpet and launches itself at me. Head bent, dressed all in black. There's a blur of movement, and a blade whines through the space.

I slide aside.

The breeze displaced by the stranger shimmers over my neck. A flash of pain cuts through me as the blade nicks my skin.

I thrust out my leg, and the intruder goes sprawling to the floor, only to turn in a move which should have been near impossible.

It calls attention to the lithe lines of the body that is wrapped in that jumpsuit. The figure launches itself back at me, and I bend my knees and throw the intruder over my shoulder.

There's a thump, then the sword skitters across the wooden floor.

I swivel around and close the distance to where the infiltrator leaps up from the center of the carpet.

The colors fade, the room shrinks around me. My vision narrows in on the face, to where the dark cloth has unraveled from around the head of the newcomer. Eyes of shattered green blaze at me.

The hair on my nape rises.

It's her, the woman from my dreams.

A strand of dark-red hair slinks free.

The scent of rain on cool dawn air bleeds through the space, interlaced with that sugary essence of slickness.

Blood rushes to my groin.

Every instinct inside me goes on alert. "Omega," I rasp.

# 2

Lucy

I lift my chin, then farther up, then all the way up, to meet his gaze. To call the General massive is an understatement. He is a monster. A man-mountain, the biggest, most powerful alpha I have ever seen.

His blue eyes blaze at me.

A ripple of fear mixed with something else—lust? Anticipation? — tightens my stomach.

His face is all hard planes and dark angles. Long black hair flows to his shoulders. His lower lip is full, obscenely so. It should soften his looks; instead, it only heightens the sense of danger that clings to him like a rich coat.

It's the exact opposite of the faded vest that embraces his torso.

His clothes strike a jarring note in the middle of the most prosperous pocket of this city, which is where we are, but it suits this alpha. Declares exactly what he is: an asshole who doesn't give a damn about anyone else.

Who takes pleasure in surprising his friends and outwitting his enemies —no, he doesn't have friends…doesn't need friends…or lovers or… How would he be as a lover? A dominant? A male who'd take without mercy? That feminine, omega core of me quivers in anticipation.

A pulse flares to life between my thighs.

An age-old instinct deep inside awakes…and insists this alpha will pleasure me. He'll bite me, lick me, suck me…and a piercing wave of desire twists my stomach.

Heat flushes my skin, and yet I feel cold, so cold.

I try to take a step forward, but my feet feel weighed down.

The alpha thrusts out his chest, and the force of his dominance crashes over me.

My breath catches.

I can't move. Can't think. Can't do anything but stare at his face, drink in his features. Open my heart and absorb every last particle of impact that his sheer charisma has on me.

I want to trace that long, hooked nose of his. To close the distance between us and bite his square, pronounced jaw. Lick it, nibble on it, then pull his head down between my thighs until his hard whiskers rub across my sensitive core.

Heat floods my skin.

My nipples tighten.

I don't need to look down at my breasts to know they're thrusting out, their sharp edges a palpable outline against the material.

He must know the effect he has on me, for the strong cords of his throat ripple. His sculpted chest seems to widen as he straightens and plants his arms on his trim hips. His powerful shoulders block out the sight of the room. His entire presence sucks up the air in the space. The strength of his personality is a visceral force that crashes into me and threatens to overpower me. I want to reach for the throbbing space between my legs and relieve the pressure that is building in my womb. What is happening to me?

"Do you know what I do to those who challenge me?" He growls.

The rich sound grates over my sensitized nerve endings and shudders straight to my center.

My thighs quiver, my stomach trembles, and I thrust my pelvis forward in blatant invitation. What the hell? It seems my body has already arrived at a decision and the rest of me is struggling to catch up.

I grit my teeth. "I am sure you are going to tell me." Every instinct in me tells me to cower…to give in to him. But I cannot. Will not. The part of me that is honed to fight back, insists I resist.

I jut out my chin.

My heart pounds in my rib cage, and a pulse flares to life between my thighs.

He growls again, and the sound tugs at my nerves. The vibrations roll over me and surround me. Cocooning me in the center.

It's like nothing I have ever heard before.

Moisture pools in my core. The scent of slick bleeds into the air. I gasp. No, not now. I can't be heading straight into a heat cycle, not when I am here on a mission. Is it the adrenaline of the attack that has brought on this sudden wave of need?

His lips, those sensuous lips, tighten.

A vein throbs at his temple, and his cheeks flush as he looks down at me from his superior height.

I should feel emboldened that I am having an effect on him, the most powerful alpha in all the land, but instead a writhing need to challenge him tears at me. To ask him. To give in to his every demand. And that confuses me.

"You are an omega but not a submissive?" He frowns.

The hackles of my neck rise. I had not expected this alpha to figure that out.

Genetic mutation brought on by climate change has divided the human race into three subspecies: alphas, betas, and omegas, and I happen to belong to the weakest of them. But the warring sides of my personality have made me an anomaly in this world where alphas take, and omegas are raised with the expectation of being bred.

"It's why you should let me go. I am not suitable for reproduction." My stomach trembles, my palms begin to sweat. I am trying to rationalize with a savage.

Accelerated cellular transformation over the past few generations has equipped the alphas with the ability to knot the omegas and increase the chance of impregnation.

As for omegas, the onset of heat cycles at puberty compel most to seek out an alpha to rut them through it. Nature's way of balancing out the dwindling population count, helped by the fact that heat suppressants are banned. Even black market supplies of the precious chemicals have run out.

I'd managed to hide myself away during the worst of these phases, had never felt compelled to lay with any alpha, not until this monster.

I need him, yet I want to fight him.

I must show him he can't just take. Not without paying a price first. Not without begging, pleading, making me scream.

Anticipation stretches my belly.

An age old instinct inside me jolts to life. My core clenches. My knees quake, and I push my boot-clad feet into the dirt for purchase.

He angles his head and peels back his lips. "On the contrary, it renders the entire process so much more interesting."

There is so much cruelty in his look...so much lust...so much everything.

My skin tightens.

Every single emotion that I have fought against my entire life, denied myself, all of it drips from his gaze.

I can't tear my gaze away.

I clench my fingers, my muscles strain, and I try, once more, to move. It only sends another pulse of pain through me. Being in this particular alpha's presence is weighing me down, making me feel like I am already in his control.

How is that possible?

The General takes a step forward, and his scent slams into me. Earthy, woodsy, and liberally laced with pheromones.

I am sure he can see every single emotion, every nuance of the feelings that tremble over me right now.

My belly clenches. My womb spasms. Slick pools between my legs and slides down my inner thighs.

His nostrils flare. He leans back on his heels. One side of his lips rises in a smirk.

The alpha knows exactly what he wants. His eyes gleam. His features flush.

Fear twists my insides. My limbs tingle.

It's as if I am watching everything unfold in front of me from a distance.

Setting my jaw, I square my shoulders, only for another burst of pain to radiate out from my center.

I arch my back, thrust my breasts out at the keening need that grips me.

I wrap my arms around my waist and cannot stop the groan that ripples up my throat. Even to my own ears it feels more like an invitation, a call to the alpha to do what he was born to do to an omega. To mate me, knot me, and make that pain inside me go away.

To fill that emptiness that is once again writhing, gnawing, and tearing at me, growing inside me with every passing millisecond until it feels like I am one big mass of yearning that will not stop. Not until he slams into me, and no, no, no! This can't be happening.

I'd starved myself of food for days to weaken my libido; I'd also calculated the time of the month to make sure I am between heat cycles. I hadn't counted on the proximity to this particular alpha sending me straight into one.

My head spins with the overload of endorphins that my overwrought nervous system is dumping into my blood. All brought on by his presence. Him. He's the reason why my body is responding with such primal need. The omega in me recognizes him. Only him.

My pulse thuds in my head; my vision blurs.

Pain cramps my womb, and I double over.

The shortage of omegas has led to alphas exploiting them, taking them at will. As he no doubt intends to overpower me now.

I will not let him do that. I straighten in time to see the General stalk toward me. His masculine presence tugs at my nerves, pushes down on my skin, sinks into my blood. My head spins.

Heat sweeps over my skin and heads to my lower belly. My core weeps.

All of my life I have tried to deny that I am an omega: the receiver, the nurturer whose insides are ravenous for an alpha's touch, who has been deprived of the sensory stimulation that only comes from an alpha's rut. Now, his scent, that concentrated testosterone, sinks into my blood, forcing a reaction.

The General growls.

It's a long, drawn-out purr that seems to emerge from the very depths of his masculine body.

The hair on my neck stands on end.

Liquid need radiates out from my womb, bleeds through my skin, and flares up in the air around me.

My womb cramps, and a fresh burst of slick gushes down between my legs to wet my pants. I don't dare look down, don't dare acknowledge the liquid pooling under me.

I should be mortified, ashamed at my public display of what I am...an omega meant to be mated and bred, who cannot physically hold back her reaction, not in the presence of this prime male specimen, and yet the survivor in me says I need to fight. Fight! My shoulders shudder, and I straighten my spine.

The General slams his fist to his chest. "Leave us," he roars.

The aggression comes off him in waves, surrounding me, cocooning me. Is he trying to shield me from the sight of his own men?

Footsteps sound, then fade away. Of course they'd rush to obey him. No one will dare stand up to him, and I'd walked into this predator's lair and challenged him. Sweat beads my palms.

The doorway to the warehouse slams shut. The echo resounds through my head. The blood thumps at my temples. A pulse flares to life between my legs.

"You scared?" His voice bleeds through the space.

"What do you think?" I grit my teeth.

"I think I am going to enjoy breaking you." He peels back his lips, and my knees tremble. The fine hair on my nape stands up.

The scent of my fear is so strong I am sure he can smell it, and that's not good. The first sign of weakness and this dominant alpha hole will pounce. My belly twists. A flare of heat tugs low below. No, that should not excite me. The thought of him delivering on his earlier promise should not make my thighs clench in anticipation.

I need to get away from that lethal, coiled, powerful male, before he senses how his nearness is affecting me.

I stagger away from him only for my feet to tangle in the carpet, and I cry out. I go sprawling on my back and stay there.

"Get up," he snarls.

I blink then slap my palms onto the carpet for leverage and stagger back to standing. Thrusting my chin forward, I meet his gaze. Those startling blue eyes burn into me. Concentric circles of aquamarine, teal and a wild blue, that draw me in. Trapping me in the sphere of his influence.

"Kayden sent you to kill me."

My chin quivers, and I ball my fists at my sides.

His jaw firms. "I should kill you for daring to burst into my stronghold and trying to assassinate me—"

"But you won't." Yeah, that would be too merciful of him.

He's a monster, and I don't expect any pity from him. But every alpha has an ego. And this predator more than anyone else I have met. Perhaps I need to appeal to that?

He tilts his head. "Feisty, aren't you?" His voice is soft, almost casual.

My stomach churns. Whatever he has in mind for me, it's not good. The thoughts skitter through my head, and I force my brain cells to knit the words together in a coherent sequence.

"You bet." I set my jaw.

His gaze narrows.

My stomach twists, and not only with arousal. My heart hammers, and a bead of sweat trickles down my spine.

"You are a big powerful alpha. Me, I am but a helpless omega." I flutter my eyelashes.

So, I am overdoing this, he's going to see right through my act. "Why don't we make this more exciting for you?" I force out the words through a throat gone dry.

He angles his head.

Guess what? He bought it. A flicker of hope sparks in my chest.

Then his lips widen in a smile, and it's so feral, I know, he's not going to let me go. Not that easily. There's a heavy feeling in the pit of my stomach. My heart thuds, and I almost lose my will to resist—almost.

"I agree." He thrusts out his chest.

"Huh?"

Why am I having this conversation with him? I am only delaying the inevitable, that's all, but I have to try, have to.

"Run." His nostrils flare, "I'll even give you a head start. You have until I count to ten."

"What do you mean?" I gulp down a breath.

"You are losing precious seconds."

No, it can't be. This is not exactly what I'd had in mind when I had suggested making things more exciting. Not.

"Nine."

The alpha is toying with me? He's going to hunt me? My palms sweat. It can mean only one thing. He wants to increase the anticipation of whatever is to come. The violence, the ultimate conclusion to this game is only one, and it's not going to be in my favor.

I close my fists so tightly my nails slice into my skin. The scent of copper leaks into the air.

"On the other hand, perhaps you'd rather we conclude this farce right now?" His eyes gleam.

The bastard no doubt thinks I don't have a chance of outrunning him. I square my shoulders and thrust out my chest. I will not submit, not so easily.

His gaze sweeps over my breasts, down to my core, and he stares at the space between my legs. There's no mistaking the anticipation that laces his features.

I want to scratch that look of satisfaction off his face, to deny that my insides tremble in response. More moisture gathers between my legs. What is wrong with me? I am here to kill him. Not to mate him. Not. To. Mate. Him.

My pulse races.

I turn on my heels so fast I almost stumble, then find my balance. A scream boils up, and I bite down on my lips to hold it back.

"That the best you can do?" His voice mocks me.

My legs feel weak, yet I force myself to move, to put one foot in front of the other. Keep going. Don't stop.

Reaching the exit of the warehouse, I throw myself against the doors.

# 3

Zeus

The double doors swing open, and she races through, leaving behind the sugary scent of her slick. The spicy scent of her fear leaks into the air, laced with that spoor of the rain on cool dawn air that is so uniquely her.

My cock throbs, straining against my pants. Adrenaline pumps through my blood. I walk after her, my pace leisurely, yet everything inside pushes me to hurry. Hurry. Go after her, claim her, take her.

I've never felt such a powerful need as this to have an omega. Never felt this overwhelming urge to shield her from the gaze of other alphas, to hide her from sight until I have had my way with her. I speed up my steps and walk out into the wilderness surrounding the warehouse.

Ethan and Sol stand on either side of the doors, their gaze trained on the figure weaving through the trees.

One of the other alphas breaks formation to run after her.

"Stop."

He halts and, his shoulders bunch. The fucker angles his body to face me over his shoulder, and his torso leans forward. Every muscle in the man's body is coiled. "You don't intend to keep her all to yourself now, do you, half-breed?"

"That's General half-breed to you." I stalk over to him.

The man turns his gaze to follow the omega who is now almost out of sight. "You'll give her up to the omega harem, and then I am going to rut her and mark her and—"

Reaching him, I wrap my fingers around his neck and squeeze. The alpha is bulked up to the point of being almost obese with muscle. But I am taller than him, and while I am leaner, I know I am more powerful, and that's not ego, just a fact.

The man gasps, "Surely you are not going to kill me over an omega."

"Wrong comment." I increase the pressure of my grip, hear that sweet snap as his spine breaks. I remove my hold on him, then tap his forehead. His body tumbles over.

I walk over the body of the fallen alpha. "No one hunts her but me."

Ethan stiffens behind me, but he doesn't protest. "Of course, General."

Not that his agreement fools me.

My second has questions, but he'll table it for later. Much later if I have my way with the omega. "Make sure there's food and water in my suite."

"As you wish." Ethan's voice has an edge to it this time. He knows what I have in mind and is not happy about it. Big fucking deal.

He's this close to insubordination, and I need to tell him off. My second is not indispensable, and it's time he realized it. But right now, I have more pressing things to take care of.

"One." I complete the countdown.

Adrenaline pumps through my blood. The thrill of the chase kicks in, and I take off after her.

Heart hammering, pulse-pounding, my feet slam into the dirt, and mud flies up behind me. Reaching the end of the path, I follow the still fresh scent of her sugary essence and that unmistakable trace of fresh rain that sinks straight to my blood. My cock throbs. Warmth floods my chest. My fingers tingle with the need to touch her. I follow the trail to the pool of water in the center of the forest surrounding the stronghold.

She swam across it, in a bid to dissipate her scent and throw me off. Clever omega.

She can fight and she knows how to evade a hunter—this is not an ordinary submissive on my hands. She's unlike any woman I have ever met, someone who challenges me, faces up to me.

My groin tightens.

I quicken my pace and run around the perimeter of the pool. Her scent fades on the other side. Where could she have gone? I scan the area. Trees line the edge of the open lawns that lead down to the parapet walls. The water of the Thames River glimmer beyond that.

I run towards it, calculating how far she could have gone. It wouldn't be like her to do the obvious and hide in the forest on the far side of the stronghold. This way is more exposed, more dangerous. It's exactly the route she'd take.

I run across the grass, straight through the last line of trees.

There's a rustle from the branches above, and that sweet scent of her pours over me. My instincts scream at me to swerve; every part of me stiffens to alertness. But if I were to move aside, she'd hit the ground. The thought of that soft body being hurt, being marked by anything else except my fingers sends a primal burst of anger through me.

She slams into me from above.

The force of it topples me on my back. And then she is on me, her legs squeezing my waist, her fingers around my throat.

"Round one is mine, alpha-hole." She pants then rams her forehead down on mine.

Sparks of red and white flare behind my eyes, pain shoots through my head, but already I am moving. "Not yet, omega-*hole*." I bare my teeth, grab her waist—she's so small that both my palms meet on either side—and then I twist my body so she's lying under me, her strong thighs still gripping my waist, her ankles locked around my back. I bend over her.

Her cheeks flush; her chest heaves.

I push my arousal against her core. It's a blatant sign of who is more dominant, not that there is any doubt about that, okay? Still, it doesn't hurt to show her who's in charge here, does it?

Her gaze widens, her lips part, and fuck! I want to lean down and slide my tongue into that ripe mouth even as I ram my cock balls deep into her pussy.

She must sense my intention, for that sweet, sugary scent of her slickness leaks into her air.

"Does the thought of being taken by me turn you on, Omega?" I lower my voice to just short of a purr, holding back the rich sound that I already know will arouse her further.

Her eyelashes flutter. She swallows, and her hips wriggle under me, brushing against my iron-hard shaft.

Heat bursts through my veins, radiating through my blood, until it feels like every part of me is on fire, with need. For her.

She thrusts out her breasts, and her nipples are outlined through the material of her tight black T-shirt, so sharp, so enticing.

"Oh, Alpha, please take me, rut me."

She flicks out her tongue to lick her lips, and I feel it all the way down to the tip of my shaft.

"Said not this omega." She bares her teeth.

With a move I don't see coming—and I have faced down some of the best hand-to-hand fighters in this land and won—she twists her body, then makes to slide out from under me. I let her go until she is sure she is almost free. Almost. I wait until her features relax, then snake out my arms. I grab her wrists, and twist them up above her head, shackling her there.

A growl rips out of me and her gaze widens. The green of her iris lightens. The scent of her arousal deepens. A pulse tics to life at my temples. My cock throbs in tandem.

I hold her down with my more powerful body, and this time there is no finesse. Only brute force. An alpha laying claim to his omega. "Oh, you will be begging for a lot more before I am done." I take her mouth.

I had meant to punish her for what she'd done. Not the physical hurt when she'd rammed her head against mine. It's my ego that is more bruised —the one that cannot accept that this sprite of an omega could have flounced into my stronghold and then attempted to kill me. It's that which makes me ram my tongue between her lips and swirl it over her teeth, and then I suck in her essence.

Honey and melting ice and sweet, tangy berries, the taste goes straight to my head. I growl low in my throat. The sound rips out of me. Possessive, harsh, it rolls over her. Her entire body seems to stiffen, then relaxes.

Her thighs quiver.

I smell the dampness of her slick, wetting her pants and sinking into the seams of my crotch. My dick throbs, needing to be inside of her.

I transfer her wrists to one hand and sweep the other palm down the side of her arm, to her breast, squeezing that ripe nipple.

I feel the shudder flow down her side as her pelvis thrusts up to cradle my hardness.

Another growl wells up from me, rippling over where her breasts are crushed against the planes of my chest. The sugary scent of her arousal is all around me. I slide my hand down her hips to squeeze the lush curves of her butt. Mine. All mine.

Her body arches under me, her spine curves, the cradle of her hips calls to me. All her muscles shudder, and it's so fucking hot. A primal need grips me. My shoulders go solid.

I slide the heel of my hand between us to rub against her core, her still-fabric-covered center, needing to feel that slickness, wanting to lick it up, pushing, shoving, cupping her core, dry humping her with my hand. Wanting to see her come.

A low moan bleeds up her throat. Her teeth dig into my lower lip, and shock waves ricochet down my spine.

"Fuck, Omega." I tear my mouth from hers.

"Not yet." She twists her body, wrenches her wrists from my grip, and slides out from under me. This time she breaks free.

# 4

Lucy

The alpha of alphas had all but fucked me right here in the open, and I had let him.

Not that it should come as a surprise, him trying to take me right here in the open without finesse. It's exactly what I'd expect of a brute like him.

But my response to him, the way I had opened my mouth, my legs… my heart…no, not that, not yet, but if I let him, he could get under my skin, and what am I thinking about?

He's treating me like I am a caged animal. To him I am another omega he can drag off to his lair and rut and—my belly tightens—I want him to do it.

I want him to reach down and place his lips where his hand had been between my legs. I need to feel his tongue thrust inside me, feel that thick shaft whose length had throbbed against my waist, fill me, take me, knot me. "Fuck." I scream more to hear the sound of my own voice, so I can try to shake off this sexual haze that has gripped me. This need that twists my insides, that makes me want to turn away and retrace my steps and throw myself at him.

"No. Fucking. Way." I will not let him capture me.

I push my feet into the ground, focus my eyes on my goal. The wall, get to the wall.

My belly clenches; my skin heats.

The thud of his footsteps draws closer, as he chases after me. The scent of burned pinewood pours over me. His scent. So evocative, so potent. It's laced with the tangy spoor of his arousal. It sinks into my blood, and my core clenches.

Goosebumps flare over my skin. "Keep going," I swear to myself, then blink the sweat from my eyes. I hit the wall and clutch at it. My hands slip on the surface, and I almost scream out in frustration.

"Stop, Omega." His voice is low, resonant, and it slides over my skin, incessant, incandescent.

It calls to me.

"No." I shove my hand over the top of the wall, and this time find purchase. I haul my body over it, almost go over the side, then at the last second straighten myself to stand poised on the narrow length.

"Don't do this." His voice is soft, so tempting. So enticing. I hear the promises hidden in the tone and don't dare turn. If I do, I'll be lost.

I grip the surface with my boots, stand there balanced on the wall, trying not to stare at the churning mass of water far below. The wind blows over me, and I sway with it, trying to keep my balance.

The breeze cuts off, and I know he's there behind me. His big body is shielding me from the elements. And it shouldn't feel like he's trying to protect me. But it does, and that doesn't make sense.

"Turn around, Omega."

I shake my head, glance at the other side of the river. Can I swim across? That's assuming I survive the fall. I glance down at the water and mistake!—my knees quake. I lose my balance, doubling over all the way from my waist. My heart pounds, my leg muscles scream in protest, then I straighten again.

There's silence behind me. I don't see him, don't hear him. His scent fades away, and I miss it already. I miss his presence. How bizarre is that?

How can you miss something you've never had?

I've never had anyone watch out for me, not until now. But he isn't my protector. He's an alpha who'd take me and rut me, and my heart stutters. The horrible thing is that I want him to.

I don't want to die without knowing what it is like to have an alpha's cock—not any alpha, *this* alpha. *His* shaft. I need it inside me, and what does that make me? Another omega who is driven by her needs. Yeah, that's all I am. But maybe, if I take the plunge and dive into the water…I can redeem myself. Perhaps this is the way to prove to myself that I am not just a pussy driven to find fulfillment in the arms of an alpha. A man I hadn't met until less than half an hour ago.

A low purr bleeds through the air. It loops around me, surrounds me, sinks into my blood. Warms me, enfolds me, caresses me.

How is it possible for one single consonant to carry so many complex notes, so much need?

I feel myself sway, feel my muscles relax, even as the still thinking part of my mind screams at me to fight. Fight. I half-turn, shuffling my feet, on the wall. Pieces of gravel slide off and over the side.

"Look at me." His voice is soft and insistent, and yet there is a trace of steel running through it. "Now."

The dominance in his tone cuts through the thoughts swirling around in my head, and slams into my chest. It pushes down on my shoulders, tugs at my nerves, forcing me to obey.

I lift my gaze to his.

Find myself drawn into those deep-blue eyes. So calm, so serene, so false, and yet so true. So intense. Deeper than the water behind me. Brighter than the skies above.

Standing on the wall, I am about level with that gaze.

Another low purr rumbles up his chest, his throat, pours out of his mouth, and I sway toward it. Toward that massive chest that can take my weight. A dense cloud of heat spools off his body and slams into me. I gasp.

My insides churn, my toes curl, everything in me insists I close the space between us, that I throw myself at him, rip off his clothes, feel his naked skin, lick the sweat that drips down his throat and ask him to take me. Right now.

This is insane.

There is a buzzing in my ears. I shake my head to clear it, then stagger back, taking a step away from him, and into space. I fling out my hand, and then there's only the whine of the breeze.

# 5

Zeus

Her gaze widens, and then her body begins to fall. My heart slams against my rib cage. I leap across the distance that covers us and, leaning over, grab at her hand. I close my fingers around her wrist.

The weight of her body pulls me over the side. I hook my foot under the space at the bottom of the wall for leverage. She is not very heavy, yet my arm feels like it's being pulled out of my socket. Sweat beads my forehead. Her body sways in the breeze. Her features tighten, and the color slides from her face. Still, she doesn't scream, doesn't panic. That surprises me and turns me on. She's fucking strong, doesn't scare easily, and I can't wait to break her.

It's even more important that I save her.

I strengthen my stance and then take a step back. Flexing my biceps, I heave her up. All the while, I hold her gaze. Those green eyes of hers stare at me; in their depths is a grim determination.

She actually thought she could have survived the fall and escaped, and perhaps she might have, but if I have my way, it will be a while before she sees any open space. Not until I have shown her who is her master. Not until I have taken her body and soul. Not until I own her thoughts, know her feelings, can second-guess her every move. Not until every part of her is mine. Only *mine.*

I don't realize I have spoken the word aloud until her gaze widens. I can see the exact moment it sinks in about who is her rescuer. Her green pupils dilate. With fear? Arousal? Then, she kicks out her legs and pulls me over, almost all the way over the side.

Once again, I press my feet into the ground to find purchase. Then, hanging over the side of the parapet, I fling out my other arm to grab her shoulder.

"Let me go." She snarls at me, holding my gaze.

"Never." I bare my teeth, widen my stance, and yank her up.

The leverage pulls her up and over the side, and the weight of her body crashes into me. This time I am prepared. I heave her over my shoulder and then, swiveling around, I race up the lawns. I need to get her to where she is safe, where she can't harm herself like that again.

She squirms in my hold and I sense her draw in a breath. All her muscles tense. Oh! No, she is not going to escape, not this time.

I tighten my hold and squeeze her thighs into my chest. Reaching the staircase, I race up the steps two at a time.

She begins to struggle harder, wriggling in my grasp. Each twitch of her hips only bleeds more of that omega scent of her arousal into the air. My cock hardens so much that it makes me stumble and almost fall, and fuck, I've had enough. Something inside me snaps. I slap her butt, once, twice, a third time. I intend to hurt. Intend to quieten her, need to feel that curved flesh give under my palm, feel that firmness resist. My fingers curl with the need to feel her naked skin slide against mine.

She stills.

I fling open the double doors to my suite and stride in. The sound of the bolt crashing home echoes around the space.

"No, no. No." She punches a fist against my side.

Damn but she doesn't give in, does she? A part of me relishes the fact that she still resists me. It's going to make her submission so much sweeter.

She sinks her teeth into my back, and the sharp edges graze the skin through my vest. I feel it all the way to the tip of my cock.

Hell, I've been hard from the second I set eyes on her. She'd charged me, armed with nothing but that puny knife and had drawn blood. She'd taken me by surprise.

When was the last time anyone had managed to do that? Not since I had dueled with Ethan, and we'd been teenagers then. *And Kayden had sent her.* Had he anticipated that this omega would get through my defenses much easier than any alpha would?

A prickle of awareness tugs at my subconscious, and I push it aside. Not even Kayden could have expected this omega getting as far as she has.

It should piss me off really that she thinks she can go toe to toe with me, and yet it's alluring. And exciting. She is wild, this one. She will not give in easily. Her audacity is an aphrodisiac that calls to me. And there is no way I am letting her out of this room, not for a long time.

She knows it, too.

And perhaps it is that which makes her struggle afresh.

She snarls and tries to knee me in the groin. I swerve, and her leg scrapes my waist, her inner thigh brushing my hardness. The scent of her arousal is heavy in the air. Honeyed, yet with a hint of something deeper… I have no doubt she will taste sweeter.

Desire tightens my groin.

She slams her fist into my back. The vibration shudders through me. I don't stop the growl that escapes my throat and am rewarded with her body trembling against mine.

It's cute that she thinks I will actually heed her cries, that I might consider setting her free. Not when she'd walked right into the den of the big bad alpha. I angle my head and sink my teeth in the curve of her butt.

She screams out. "You bit me?"

"*You* bit me first," I growl. "I only returned the favor."

She thrashes her legs, her body bucks, and she pounds her fists on my back.

"Behave." I drag my arm down to below her hips and hold her there.

"You haul me away, capture me and bring me here, and you expect me to stay quiet?" Her voice is muffled, but I still hear her.

Her knees dig into my waist.

"I gave you a chance to escape, you failed. You are mine." I snap my teeth.

She trembles.

A primitive surge of satisfaction tightens my groin. She's afraid. Good. "It seems it's finally sinking in you are in my control." I sneer.

She brings down her joined fists on my back. The blow only sends another pulse of heat tearing through my veins.

"Have you lost touch with reality so much that you don't know right from wrong anymore?"

There's a touch of anguish in her voice and helplessness, and it tugs something inside me. Some long-forgotten, humane part of me that only one other woman has ever touched. What am I doing? I'd seen her and lost control. Had smelled that essence of ripe omega mixed with a dash of something forbidden, something so tangible that I had wanted to throw her down on the floor and rut her right there in the open.

It had blinded my senses to everything else. Except her. I am the hunter. She is my spoils. So why am I so hesitant? I cross the floor toward my bed.

She must realize that I am approaching my destination for she begins to struggle again. Arms and leg thrashing, she writhes in my grasp.

Another flare of her arousal hits me, and on cue, my cock thickens. What the fuck? I tighten my grip on her, "Keep that up and I won't be responsible for what happens to you. I've been a gentleman so far."

"You are kidding, right?" She yells, "If this is how you treat your guests—"

"That's where you are mistaken." I reach the bed. "You aren't a guest. And I am not your host."

I am a callous bastard who does not hesitate to plunder first and ask questions later, as she's going to discover soon enough.

She knees me in the stomach, and the breath whooshes out of me. Another shudder of arousal tightens my belly.

"Let me go," she pleads.

"You bet." I throw her down on the mattress.

She bounces once, then springs up on her feet. Of course, she does. She's already demonstrated that she knows how to fight, and she'd almost held her own…almost, even against someone as powerful as me. And that's not ego, just a fact.

It's imperative that I make her a conquest. My dick throbs. The beat echoes the pulse thudding at my temples.

Swiveling around, I stomp to the table by the window and stab my finger at the tray of food there. "Eat." I jerk my chin at the omega.

Her features grow pale. Her gaze drops to the tray, and she purses her lips. "I don't want to eat, you fool."

Her choice of insult is almost anticlimactic.

I snicker, and the skin at the corners of her eyes tightens.

Still holding her gaze, I kick off my boots. "In that case, let's fuck."

# 6

Lucy

Bastard! He knows that pronouncement while not exactly a surprise is only going to alarm me, and that is his intention: to frighten me so that I'll submit to him like a nice docile omega. Well, he's got that so wrong. I am not going down, not without a fight. The alpha-hole can go screw himself if he thinks I am going to make this easy on him.

He shrugs out of his vest, then places it over the chair near the bed.

The arrogance of the brute! He turns his back on me. I bare my lips, then lean low to charge him.

He tears off his tunic to reveal his naked back.

My breath catches, and my thigh muscles freeze.

Without his clothes, this alpha is overpowering.

I swallow, and my heart hammers.

Nothing has prepared me for those shoulders that seem hewn out of stone. His biceps flex, and I don't need to touch them to know they'll be hard and ungiving, like the rest of that body he is so casually baring to my gaze. Colored ink marks one side of his back and continues up and over his shoulder.

This is when I throw myself at him and catch him unawares. When he is the most vulnerable. I force my brain to connect my thoughts with action and place one trembling foot in front of the other.

He bends and pulls off his pants.

The scent of him, that earthy, woodsy, packed-with-need aroma intensifies. It's laced with something deeper, the tang of his precum, all of which sinks into my blood and heads straight to my core.

My throat closes; my mouth goes dry. Moisture seeps out from between my thighs.

The muscles of his back ripple, the intricate tattoos on his skin undulate like the patterns on a rattlesnake.

The man is deadlier. He'll hypnotize me, seduce me, take me, and I'll not be able to protest. A shiver runs down my spine.

He drapes his fatigues over the seat, and all thought dribbles out of my head. His corded flanks are a thing of beauty that sweep down to meet the backs of those muscled thighs.

I must have made some noise, for he turns and gives me a full-frontal view of that sheer unleashed dominance of his physical self.

His chest is sculpted. There are tattoos colored across those angles and planes. His honeyed skin sweeps over a torso that has weathered many fights. A tattoo slashes diagonally across the expanse, and I want to touch it. Trail my fingers over those pecs, down to where his concave stomach dips to meet his shaft. His fully aroused massive dick that stands up almost vertical with need.

Heat sweeps through my body, chased by chills. Goosebumps flare on my forearms. Every pore of my skin seems to open as if to absorb each nuance of his touch, the feel of him. My body is preparing for the invasion by this alpha that is bound to come. My stomach lurches. I want to look away but I can't.

I want to move but my body feels too heavy.

A ripple of need pierces my core.

I want to taste him. Want to lap up the seed that drips from him and rub it all over myself.

I can almost feel that slithery moisture trickling over me. The sensations twist my insides. My thighs clench and a low, keening need rocks my belly.

His gaze narrows and those blue eyes seem to lighten into colorless mirrors that amplify my own desires before throwing them back at me.

My skin chafes with the need to go to him, to throw myself at him and rub my skin over his.

He holds his arms loosely at his sides, then widens his stance. I can see every last nook and hollow of that beautiful, delectable, hateful body.

The cords of his strong throat flex, the planes of his chest rippling as if there is an unseen force unfurling inside him.

The brute is preening for me, making sure I know exactly who is going to possess me. A powerful dominant alpha male who will take without mercy.

I should back away, scream, try to plot on how to get out of there. But that omega core of me insists I am exactly where I should be. The need to draw into myself, and make myself smaller is overwhelming. I will not do that. To do that will only give him an advantage. I jut out my chin and stay where I am.

His jaw firms. Then, he angles his head and studies me. His gaze is brooding, calculating, stained with lust and a strange cruelty.

My throat closes. My fingers tingle and the hair on my nape hardens. Why doesn't he do something? Say something? Anything to break the silence that fills the room and presses down on my shoulders. Sweat beads my palms.

The chiseled planes of his chest tense, tightening his skin that is the color of honey. I want to run my lips over the demarcation of those powerful pecs, to lick and suck my way down to those thighs shaped from sheer muscle and tendons and covered with a smattering of light hair. The chafing of his rougher skin on mine would set off delightful trails of friction over my belly, leaving tracks of redness where they'd scrape the insides of my thighs.

Sparks of heat jolt through my chest.

The tension in the room ratchets up, and my nerves feel like they are being strained to the breaking point. Every part of me feels like it is on fire, yearning for his touch, yet he stays unmoving. He could be a sculpture or an obscene dedication to everything that is lethal.

My eyelids feel too heavy, and I lower my gaze back to where that massive shaft throbs. In the last few seconds, his shaft has grown bigger, harder.

My breath stutters. He's too large, too massive. Every part of him screams that he is bent on dominating me, that he will not stop until he gets what he wants, and not even then. Not until every single inch of my skin bears his imprint.

Something very much like anticipation grips me. The still rational part of my brain screams out a warning.

I need to get out of here.

Out of these clothes which feel too tight on me. Out of these barriers which I have imposed on myself. Tear through the walls and expose that giving, needing omega inside me.

The yearning is so primal that my womb cramps and slick gushes down my inner thighs. I wrap my arms around my waist and groan.

The sound seems to turn him on even more, and his already engorged shaft thickens further.

He takes a step forward, and I have no doubt that he is going to close the distance between us. He is going to lick up the sweat from between my breasts, then thrust his tongue inside my pussy and absorb my essence, and the awful thing, the beautiful thing is that I can't wait. I need him to take the choice out of my hands and put me out of this misery.

The image cuts through the haze that the heat cycle has brought on. I straighten my shoulders and tear my gaze from the part of him that promises me the ultimate freedom.

He stalks toward me to stand at the foot of the bed.

This close, the dominance of his presence weighs down on my chest, presses down on my shoulders. The fine hairs on the nape of my neck rise. A plume of heat spools off his chest and slams into me, a moan whines out of me.

His gaze widens, those cruel lips curl in a smirk.

My sex quivers in response. Every pore on my skin pops open tuned into him, waiting for him… waiting.

He leans forward on the balls of his feet. His scent crashes over me, sinks into my blood and tugs at my nerve endings. My skin puckers.

Closer, I need him to come closer, why has he stopped? No, what am I thinking? What's happening to me? My throat closes. "Don't you dare," I gulp.

# 7

Zeus

"Don't challenge me." I keep my voice casual when every part of me aches to cover her body with mine.

Waves of fear roll from her. Yet she holds up her fists in front of her. The skin stretches white over her knuckles.

Standing on the bed that is on a raised platform, she is still not at eye level with me.

I frown. "You are tiny."

Her chest rises and falls; her thick hair curls over her face and around her neck. Red highlights gleam in it. How will it feel to have those locks wrapped around my palm as I yank back her head and close my mouth around those delectable lips?

"My looks are deceptive." She raises her head and meets my gaze.

"I said tiny...not fragile," I smirk. "Your will is strong enough that you walked into my turf and took me on, not to mention facing down a crowd of alphas. Clearly, you are also stupid."

"Stupid?" She blinks as if she can't quite believe that I said that to her face.

Hey, I did compliment her first, didn't I? Backhanded as it was, I was still appreciative of her fearlessness...or should I call it recklessness?

"Not as much as you are." She thrusts out her chin.

"Oh?" I angle my head. "Pray, tell me what you mean by that?" My voice is casual...and while my men would have given me a clear berth on hearing the threat in my voice, it seems to have the opposite effect on her.

"I'll go one better," Her shoulders tighten. The muscles of her arms bunch, and I know she is preparing to attack me.

I brace myself for the inevitable when she snaps her shoulders back, and her breasts strain against her jumpsuit. Those nipples outlined through the material tease me, call to me, begging me to cup them, massage them, curve my tongue around the hard nubs and pull on them.

All other thought goes out of my head.

Everything except that I am an alpha and this luscious omega, ripe for the plucking, going into her heat cycle, is here, in my room, in my bed. On my turf.

Fuck everything else.

My thighs go rock-hard.

Her gaze slides back down to my dick. Her little pink tongue slides out to lick her lips, and I feel the ripples of need all the way to my groin.

I have to have her now.

I growl my intention, drawing that harsh purr out, all the way from the depths of my being, up through my ribcage, pouring it out, unfurling the notes over her, lassoing her with it and pulling her closer, closer.

She groans and stutters mid-step. Her gaze widens; the black pupils in those forest-green eyes bleed out. "That's not helping."

"On the contrary. I'm making sure you are wet enough to ease my penetration."

I breathe out a low purr. And am rewarded when the sugary scent of her arousal grows deeper.

Her cheeks flush. "Thanks for painting—or should I say panting—that for me in graphic detail."

I can't stop the surprised chuckle that cracks out of me. "Not only gorgeous, and a fighter, but also smart." The compliments roll off my tongue so easily. I hear my own words and start.

Just a one-off, that's all it is.

I never waste time on words, definitely not before I fuck. Not ever. And certainly not to sing the praises of the omega who's already in my grasp. I have no need to tell her what I think of her. Really not.

Her cheeks flush. "You going to say now that your approving talk will also ease your infiltration of my body?" She huffs out a breath.

"No, actually… I am deciding how to put that sharp tongue of yours to better use." I gaze at her mouth, knowing that will only turn her on further. Somehow, my plan of taking her has turned into a full-blown seduction. It feels so right, and yet it's not what I want. Is it? I need her to fear me, lay with me, fuck me back perhaps, just as I intend to worship her body, too.

Molten heat courses through my blood.

She must sense my thoughts, for her lips tremble. Her chest heaves. She curls her fingers into fists at her sides, and I know it's because she's stopping herself from touching me.

"You want me, admit it." I run my hands over my chest.

"No." Her gaze follows my actions as I slide my palm down to my thick cock and palm it at the base. Squeezing it down the length until a drop of precum oozes out.

She licks her lips. Oh, yeah, she wants me, wants my dick inside her all right. "Why are you fighting the inevitable?"

"Because… I have sworn to only lay with my mate."

Her features freeze as if she can't believe she's blurted that out. I angle my head. Interesting. A strange warmth pools in my chest. I don't want to examine it. Don't care what it is. Nope. No way.

"So you haven't been with any other alpha?"

She squares her shoulders. "Your ability to deduce the obvious is overwhelming." She tries to sneer, but her voice trembles, spoiling the effect.

I don't need her confirmation to reaffirm what I've already sensed. She's held back from anyone else having her, and that knowledge shakes me to the core.

I want to shove her on her back, bury myself inside her, sheath my cock in the depths of that sweet omega essence right before I turn her over, then bend her and slam into her from behind, taking her in every conceivable position.

She must read the intention on my face, for she shakes her head. "No."

I peel back my lips. "Yes."

This is when she retreats, perhaps falls on her knees and submits to me —better still, lies back, opens her thighs, and stays that way. I growl low, anticipating that sweet taste of her coating my tongue, that complex, seductive omega scent rolling through my blood as I raise and lower her on my cock. I can literally feel her skin give under my fingers when she snarls and bows her head and comes at me.

For a second it is I who blinks and freezes. I stare as she charges at me. Little hellion.

I almost admire her for her fighting instinct, for that need to not give up, to fight back until the last breath, that intuition that had kept me going all through my growing years. That had brought me here to this fine suite in the palace in the richest district of the city.

I sense a kindred spirit in her. Which is why I am going to have to break her. I almost feel remorseful at that. Almost. But I have no choice. I have my plans all laid out. I haven't come all this way to let an omega derail me.

So what if she smells like sunshine and heat and that faint sugary taste of musk that hints at her arousal?

So what if she has the most beautiful, most desirable, most luscious body that I have ever encountered?

So what if given half a chance she will claw her way under my skin, rip out my heart, and trample all over it, even as she claims ownership of my soul...and I must put an end to this. To whatever spell she is casting over me. Her omega essence is clearly ensnaring me, making me lose my composure, and that I will not allow. No way.

When she rushes at me, I take the brunt of her hit. I don't feel it. No, that's a lie. The feel of her breasts sliding against my chest, the scrape of her knuckles as she smashes her fist into my side, all of it turns me on.

I don't move. And it's not the fear of hurting her that keeps me immobile. It's just that I relish the splatter of her punches on my chest until the fight finally goes out of her.

She falls to her knees, head hanging forward, shoulders slumped.

She's breathing heavily, her lips parted, her spine curved down. It's a gesture of total submission, one I appreciate.

My cock twitches and I delight in every second of the tension building in my groin. The inevitable coupling is going to be so much sweeter. So satisfying, that bite of pure satisfaction that comes with having broken an omega completely and utterly.

Reaching down, I swipe her hair away from her face, then clamp my fingers around her neck.

Her body tenses, then she springs up and snaps her head forward.

# 8

Lucy

I rear up and smash my head into his chin. Shock waves ricochet down my neck, down my spine. Sparks of red flash behind my eyes.

It feels like I've run into a brick wall. The impact slices through my body.

I cry out and fall back on the bed. Tears run down my cheeks. I'd known I wasn't going to be able to escape, knew it from the moment I'd agreed to this half-assed plan to assassinate the General, that this could go either way. But until that moment I'd not realized I'd held out a last sliver of hope that I'd be able to break out of the grasp of this alpha.

He'd given me a chance to escape, and I had failed.

Then he'd allowed me to go at him, and the one solid hit that I'd got in at him had laid me low. The physical pain from the impact rips through me. A dull pressure pushes against the back of my eyeballs. More than the fact that I am utterly and completely at his mercy, it is the humiliation that I can't hold my own against him that frustrates me. I've honed my fighting skills against some of the most skilled warriors, and all of it is to no avail.

It's strange that more than the possible rape of my body that this alpha no doubt intends, it is the rape of my pride that hurts me more.

The throbbing in my head increases in crescendo. My guts twist, and the band around my chest tightens.

Sweat drips down my back, down my forehead, creeping into the space between my eyelids, and they sting.

I squeeze my eyes shut and lie there waiting for whatever punishment he has in store for me. Knowing only to expect the worst. Every last nightmare version of what I have heard from other omegas of how alphas will take from you, tear into you to slake their thirst...all of those scenarios crowd in on my head. My shoulders hunch. Tears slide down my cheeks and dammit, but I can't stop them.

I am aware of him swooping down on me.

The world tilts as he slides his body under me, stretching out and cradling me close to his chest. There's a strange gentleness, an almost awkward reverence to how he holds me. He doesn't soothe, doesn't say anything. His arms are around me, bands of steel that tie me to him. To keep me prisoner, to stop me from escaping, no doubt. I should feel threatened...yet I am not.

There's only a relief that I can stop pretending. Is that what I have been doing so far? Pretending? The thought brings on a fresh wave of tears, and a sob racks my body, then another. Before I know it, I am holding on to the same arms that imprison me, hanging on to him for support as I bawl my eyes out.

My insides twist.

I curl up my legs and bring them close. I am wound around this man's chest like a baby clinging to her mother.

My sobs intensify. What the hell is wrong with me? This is not the time to have a full-blown breakdown. Not in the arms of my captor. Yet surrounded by the heat of this alpha's body I feel secure in a way I've never felt before, not even with my own family. I don't have many memories of my mother who died too young. My father was a warrior, the Czar of Moscow. Though I was an omega, he'd recognized the fighter in me. He'd made sure to train me. I'd been fortunate that as a member of the royal family I'd had the choice of when to mate with an alpha. I'd managed to delay it, too, until now.

The tears keep coming.

My throat is so dry I am sure I shouldn't be able to cry anymore, and yet I can't seem to stop. It's as if all the years of pent-up hatred, fear, recklessness, all of it wound inside comes bubbling up. I am falling apart, and it's in the arms of the most powerful alpha in the land. The one who will no doubt take my virginity against my will.

But even that thought doesn't stop my weeping. Nothing matters anymore. Nothing except the feel of his arms around me.

The soft growls that rumble up his chest rock my body.

The rich bass of his purring crawls up the space between us, vibrates up his throat and curls around me. Sensuous, gentle. His tone is almost sub-vocal, and yet it's unmissable. It's hypnotic. I listen to it. Am entranced by it. I hiccough once. My ears pop, and the sound grows deeper. A soothing, resonant murmur that rolls over my skin and sinks into my blood.

Each new wave of purring sets off sparks of heat in its wake. Seducing. Comforting. Like he's weaving a cocoon around me. I am caught in the wonder of this new experience.

The earthy scent of him, mixed with the dark cinnamon of his arousal, sloshes over me. I breathe it in, not aware that I am doing it, not until the hard planes of his chest bite into my cheeks. I become aware of digging my nails into his skin, which is streaked from my tears.

*My tears.*

It's so intimate. And yet it shouldn't be like this. It shouldn't feel so right when everything else is wrong, so wrong. I shouldn't be here. With him. In his bed. Enfolded in his arms. Soaking in his warmth. Reveling in that entrancing alpha scent of his, seeking out his touch…his caresses. Him. Only him.

How can I feel so much, in such little time? And for someone completely and utterly wrong for me? My eyelids grow heavy. I try to crack them open, but it's too much of a struggle. I push against his hold, knowing I should try to break free.

Another soothing purr rumbles over me, and the muscles of my shoulders unwind.

He slides his thigh between mine, but I am too weak to protest. The rough hair of his upper thigh brushes the tender skin between my legs. I was wrong. The feel of his skin on mine is not only pleasurable, it heightens the contrast between what only he can offer and the emptiness swirling inside me. Something like pain skitters down my spine.

I swallow and reach once more for that rumbling that is growing in volume, deepening around me. Pulling at me. Tugging at me. I want to protest, say something. But I feel too weak. Like I have been running, fighting too hard.

The purring changes tenor becomes deeper, resonant. It sparks a response from my nerves which immediately seem to catch fire. I shudder, not sure exactly what he's doing to me.

If this is what it means to submit, so be it.

He may as well take me when I am half out of my head with grief, with sadness, and an overwhelming desire to be done with whatever it is that an alpha does to an omega. Or not. I've heard of it but I've never been with a man before. Not because I am a prude, not for my lack of trying, but because for an omega, once you get an alpha to mate you to break the heat cycle, then you can't stop, not until the heat cycle has run its course. More often than not it results in an omega's pregnancy.

And I've never thought I'd want to bring a child into this world, not until I'd met the right alpha. Which isn't him.

My muscles tense.

His arms tighten as if he senses my discomfort.

I wriggle in his embrace, pushing against the sculpted planes of his chest.

His breath raises the hair on my head. Another purr builds up from his groin. I am lying on him so I can track exactly the source of that sound, follow it as it shivers up his iron-hard stomach, ripples through his rib cage, vibrates up his throat and then pours out in mellifluous chords that slide into my blood, straight to my core.

My thighs clench.

The soft flesh of my center quivers. A trickle of slick spurts down my inner thigh.

And it is that which brings me to being alert. Awareness tugs at my nerves. It pushes aside the haze of desire that has clogged my mind.

All of his gentleness, his tenderness, it is all a front. It has to be. A way to lull me into comfort, to make me trust, enough to allow my hormones to regroup, my core to relax and ready itself for my alpha. Which he is not; he never will be.

I raise my head, gaze at him through hooded eyelids, then lean down and sink my teeth into his neck.

# 9

Zeus

Her teeth dig into me, and the shock of it surges down my spine. There's a primitive satisfaction that she wants to own me, while a part of me cannot believe she took that liberty with me. It is my prerogative as alpha to mark her first.

Mine to own, to claim, to do with her as I want.

I've been holding back, and she has taken advantage of that; she has taken the lead in this mating game. More than the physical hurt, it's my ego that roars in protest at the liberty.

With a roar, I flip her over, pinning her to the bed.

I snag her arms together to pull them up and over her head, shackling her wrists. I want to ask her what she's trying to prove, but one look in those green eyes, and the words stutter in my mouth. I am not someone with a soft heart, I have no tenderness inside me. I take, that's what I do, yet one whiff of the fear that vibrates off her, and when I open my mouth all that emerges is a rumbling growl.

Her lips are stained by the blood she drew from me when she bit me.

It's primal, and so fucking arousing. The evidence that she already marked me, has staked her claim on me, does she realize it? It sends a fierce surge of need pounding through my veins.

My cock twitches and I grind the evidence of my arousal into her soft core—not because I want to show her how turned on I am, though that, too—but it's more a clear sign to her as to who owns her and that there is no escape from me.

"You fought well, little warrior; you can take comfort in that."

She bares her teeth, showing gums stained with my blood. "I'm not done yet." Her green eyes are so large, the pupils so dilated that it's a clear sign she is nervous, afraid, and also aroused.

"Yes, you are." Something like tenderness flushes through me. Nah. It can't be that. Me? Wanting to take care of this omega who tried to kill me? I must be losing my mind, or perhaps I have been too lenient with her. I've indulged this wildling for too long. It's time to show her the kind of pleasures only an alpha can give his omega.

I lean down and lick my blood from her lips.

Her shoulders shudder. Every muscle in her body goes on alert.

I nibble my way up her cheek to the shell of her ear, then suck on her earlobe.

She shivers. Her eyelids flutter down. A low groan spills from her lips.

"That's it, submit, give in…go with your instinct, and then it'll be easier for you."

As the words leave my mouth, her body tenses again. It seems if I speak it breaks the trance she falls into when I purr for her. And it's no hardship to do that, mind you. I'll force her if needed. I'd much prefer someone more submissive, someone more pliant, open to do my bidding… not. If that were the case, wouldn't I have taken an omega from the ones stocked in the harem, the ones my alphas lay with whenever the need to rut comes over them?

I'd done so on one occasion, but the encounter had been so unfulfilling I'd not bothered again. Then I'd caught a glimpse of that dark-red strand of her hair tumbling free of its restraint to curl over her shoulder and I'd known what was missing. Her. Her fire, her breath. Her scent. I have to have her.

My dick pulses in agreement. My shaft pushes against the softness of her core.

Her eyes fly open, and the green in them has faded to light gold. My breath stutters. She is much more breathtaking than I'd thought. It makes me want to see how the rest of her is.

What is so special about this female that she is already in my blood?

Why is this prickly omega the only one I want?

The thought pulses a trickle of discomfort down my spine. No, I have no intention of feeling anything for her. The only reason I brought her here was to punish her. To show her she can't challenge me on my own turf.

And, yeah, because the thought of any other alpha violating her is something that affects me in a way I still can't understand. It's that which makes me pull my weight off of her and stand back.

Her legs are flung apart, her breasts rising and falling, her cheeks flushed. And the remnants of the jumpsuit cling to her body like petals from a rose on damp ground.

Bending down, I grab the seam of her collar and rip the fabric to her waist. Yanking it over her legs, I pull it off her.

She is naked underneath.

Her full, lush breasts spring out, dark-pink areolae crowned with the most delicate of buds for nipples.

Desire grips me, hot and hard. I can't tear my eyes away from the perfectly formed specimen of femininity.

Her slim waist seems impossibly narrow. I trail a finger over her navel to where her waist slopes to meet the dark-red hair that points to her clit.

Goosebumps pop on her skin. Her muscles tense.

I look up to find those green eyes dilated yet burning with a fire that entrances me. She flexes her jaw. A muscle throbs above her cheekbone. She is gritting her teeth, to stop herself from making any noise, knowing that will only encourage me. And suddenly I want to hear her voice more than anything else.

I trail my finger down to the edge of her clit and hover there. Her thighs clench. Moisture trickles between her legs and pools below. The scent of her deepens and goes straight to my head.

My cock hardens and aches with the need to feel her warmth clench around me. I raise my gaze, up her trembling stomach, over her swollen breasts to her face.

Those green eyes, the gold in them sparkles and burns. Yet her lips are pursed in defiance. She is aroused. She wants me. Yet she is still able to resist me. A fierce surge of pride grips me. It makes me want her more but also slows me down. I want to seduce her until she has no choice but to give in to me. And give in she will. I've never lost a fight and don't intend to start now. Certainly not to a weaker omega.

"Does the thought of my hands on your flesh, discovering all your secrets one by one, stripping you of your layers and baring you to my gaze...does that turn you on?"

She raises her chin but doesn't answer.

She doesn't need to.

Her chest rises and falls, and her belly trembles. That sugary-sweet musk of her arousal laps at my senses.

My mouth waters.

And yet I pause and wait...for what? I can't understand my own hesitation. She is mine to take, to ruin, to do with as I want.

I am the most powerful alpha in the land, the newly ascended leader of this city.

So what stops me from having my way with this wisp of an omega who dared try to assassinate me?

Precisely nothing.

I drop to my knees and lower my mouth to that trembling flesh between her legs.

# 10

Lucy

I see the play of emotions on his face…and, really, it should not be possible to differentiate the lust that leaks from his every pore with the flicker of something very much like confusion that I am sure I glimpsed there for a second. No, surely, I am mistaken.

This is Zeus, the fiercest alpha in the city, the man who killed his own father to become the General. The very hungry male who licks his tongue from the bottom of my pussy all the way to my clit at the top.

No, no, no.

I must have said it aloud, for a low purr flows over me. This sound is tenacious, insistent, like the vocal equivalent of a battering ram, seducing me, asking to be let in. And that confuses me. I am at his mercy. He is the alpha, I am the omega, in his suite, on his bed, and his tongue is writhing inside me, and yet a part of him tries to soothe me.

I almost wish he didn't.

I wish that he'd take me and be done with it.

If it is my heat cycle that is making him want to claim me if that is all this is about, then I want him to be done with it, so I can get down to business and perhaps ask him for a way to help the rest of my omega clan. If... His fingers join his tongue in my core, stretching me, hooking inside and finding a vulnerable, delicate patch of skin that is so responsive, so delicate, so everything that I know he's found that secret place inside of me that I hadn't known existed.

I thrash my head from side to side, and my back arches off the bed, and my hands, they are buried in his hair. I should drag them away. Instead, all I can do is rake my fingernails over his scalp until they snag on his heavy locks that are...smoother than they look, silky. Like how my skin must feel in comparison to the second calloused digit he's pushed inside me.

"No, please." I moan, trying to push him—at least I think I am trying to shove him away; the fact is, I am holding his face close to my pussy and thrusting my pelvis into his face, offering up all of myself to him.

He can take me now and I wouldn't stop him.

Another deep purr from him crawls over my skin, settles in my belly.

More slick oozes from between my legs and a wave of dismay grips me. Around him, I can't control my own response. It's alarming and also makes me want to give in.

He draws in a deep breath as if he is inhaling my very essence, taking a part of me inside him. It shouldn't be so arousing, shouldn't turn me on, but it does.

Primal lust tightens my skin. I pant, only to scream when he circles his tongue over my clit, then drags it to the entrance of my channel where he licks up my moisture. Leaning up and balancing his weight on his forearms, he dribbles the liquid into my mouth. And I slurp it up from his lips and swallow it down.

I taste myself, sweet and musky, and him...spicy with a honeyed edge that is a shock. It's far from unpleasant. There's a strange intimacy in this, in tasting our joined-up essences, and it's the closest, the nearest I have ever been to anyone else. My soul seems to intertwine with his in that instant. I shake my head, trying to deny these strange feelings of heat and lust and sheer passion that are tearing me apart. It can't be like this. It can't feel so right, not when he is all wrong for me.

As if sensing my confusion, and how close I am to either submitting completely or retaliating with a fresh burst of anger, he raises his head and stares into my eyes, that startling blue gaze of his holding mine. It keeps me still for a second. I find myself slipping, sliding into those molten, colorless depths. Pulled into a strange vortex that I hadn't expected to encounter.

A jolt of awareness tugs at my nerves. Every cell in my body seems to be sensitized and yearning for his touch. The hair on my forearms harden.

I've fought enemies on the journey from my home country to get this far...but faced with the biggest monster of them all, I am speechless. A low moan swells up from the pit of my belly. I open my mouth, and all that emerges is "Please..." I gasp.

There is a flash of satisfaction in his eyes, then he leans down. The hard flesh of his shaft grazes the melting folds of my pussy. My insides twist, my belly churns...but it's not with fear. A shudder of anticipation tightens my skin. Heat enfolds me, and sweat pops on my brow.

I swallow and try to speak, but all that comes out is a mewl.

"I know." His voice is soft, so gentle, deceptively so.

My muscles relax and I spread my thighs wider. Then I raise my pelvis, a millimeter more. My core skims his swollen shaft.

He groans and rubs the head of his cock over the entrance to my throbbing channel.

A searing need sweeps over me, followed by a jolt of fear. An awareness of what I am, of what he is going to do filters into my mind. He's going to take me, and this is wrong.

This is not how I wanted it to happen for my first time.

Not with an alpha I didn't choose.

With the one who my body aches for. With the one who can match my needs. Who makes me feel this depth of yearning I'd not thought possible. I want him to break my heat cycle, I need him to fuck me, knot me, fill me with his cum, breed me. What am I thinking?

He brushes his shaft over my melting core.

His movement is almost tentative, and that is my undoing. A groan spills from my mouth. His lips fasten over mine, absorbing the sound. His hands shackle my wrists above my head, and between my legs, that vicious part of him throbs. And his mouth, oh, that hot, needy mouth of his sucks from me, drinks of my essence. It's as if he's trying to rip out the very depth of my soul and fuse it with his. I squeeze my eyelids shut and am no longer sure what I am fighting. Him? Me? This keening need that churns my gut, leaving me hungry and shaking and needy for more, so much more.

I shake my head, trying to dislodge his sensuous tongue with which he's licking the inside of my mouth.

His body shudders. He pulls back, his shoulders trembling as he props his body over mine, holding his weight up with his biceps.

And it is that unexpected gesture, the fact that he restrained himself instead of ramming into me and taking me, that has the desire roaring through my veins. Heat sears my cheeks.

I crack my eyelids open in time to see the sweat run down his temples and plop on my cheek.

His lips slow their assault, his tongue licks the inner seam of my lips... and that softer, gentler touch is so seductive, so full of promise that I tremble. In that second, he reveals a tenderness that connects with me. That omega instinct of mine rushes to the fore and tells me to grab him, hold him, take what he is offering... Do it. Even as he holds back and waits and watches me out of those searing, almost colorless eyes that mirror back my own desires.

His features are strained, his lips swollen, and yet he stays where he is.

Why is he holding back?

What is he waiting for?

Only he can give me the relief I crave. Only he can make me forget everything I have endured to come this far.

I bare my teeth and in one swift move wrap my legs around his waist and angle my hips so he slides in, a fraction more. His shaft brushes against the barrier inside me.

I shudder.

Desire pools in the pit of my stomach. Goosebumps flare over my arms. Another millimeter more...that's all that stands between this yawning emptiness and...that feeling of something I crave that I still don't understand.

His eyes flash blue with shades of a deep, dark violet in them that hints at secrets, at nightmares.

A growl rips from him.

I shiver. Then, still holding my gaze, he pulls out, all the way out of me.

# 11

———————

Zeus

I stay poised at the entrance to her moist, trembling core.

Her body heaves and bucks and strains to get closer. Her skin grazes over mine and my blood pulses with need.

That ache inside me for more, for so much more, to own her, to break her, hammers at my temples. I sniff the blood in the air, and it reminds me that it was she who had bitten me first…and yet I can't just take her.

Surprise! Apparently hidden inside is a kernel of someone decent, someone I thought I'd lost a long time ago, someone I still don't recognize. It's probably an aberration. And I am sure the restraint on my side is only because she is a virgin. No one, not even an omega who'd dared to break into my stronghold, deserves to be taken against her will for her first time.

And I *am* her first.

I grow impossibly hard at the thought. Yet I also want to watch her closely, study her reactions as she responds to my touch.

I plan to be her only. I don't question the complete, utter truth in it that I feel all the way to my core.

It was she who came to me. She, an omega on the verge of her heat cycle, knowing full well that being in the company of so many alphas was only going to drive her over the edge. She knew it…yet she had burst into my ascension ceremony. It was she who'd made the first move to claim me.

As I am going to claim her.

Slickness floods her channel, and despite myself, I slide in farther.

She groans.

So do I.

I lower my head and hover above her, balancing my elbows on either side of her body.

Her eyes are squeezed shut, and sweat beads on her upper lip.

"Look at me."

My voice comes out rough, and it feels like I have drawn it out over cut glass that lines my throat. I pinch her chin. "Open your eyes."

She must see me. Know who the alpha is who is taking her, staking his claim on her. She has to acknowledge me.

Her eyelids flutter open. Her black pupils have grown to expand, covering almost the entirety of her green irises.

More of her slick flows over my cock as I angle my hips and pause there, my stance planking over her with my weight balanced on my forearms and my feet.

A slight move and I can slide into her, ram into her all the way and give her the relief she craves. But not yet.

She moans again, fine lines appearing between her eyes. Her lips part, and her arm comes up to grip my biceps. "Please," she gnaws on her lower lip.

"Please what?"

She shakes her head and purses her mouth. Her cheeks are fiery with color. Her cheekbones stand out under her skin. Her shoulders heave, and her breasts thrust out, the nipples so hard I swear I can cut my skin on their sharpness. Desire coils and tightens my groin. I throb inside her. Every part of me wants to plow into her, to show her who she belongs to, to take her again and again. My biceps tremble with the strain of holding my weight back. "Tell me, Omega?" My jaw firms.

I move my hips and my cock scrapes the sides of her walls. A shiver of heat sparks down my spine. Her throat moves as she swallows. Her chin wobbles and her eyelids flutter down.

"Look at me," I command.

Her eyelids snap open. I hold her gaze.

"What do you want?"

Silence.

Tears lighten her eyes and tremble at the corners. I should feel remorse but I don't. All I feel is satisfaction that I moved her to this. Moved her to feel the kind of emotions I can't.

"Say it." I lower my voice, soften it so it sounds like I am cajoling her.

Why is it important that she tell me that?

Why can't I simply take her, show her that I am truly the monster everyone thinks I am? And yet somewhere deep inside, that last civilized part of me, the part that has seen my alpha father take my omega mother against her wishes, that part that had known it was wrong even then, resists.

Even as every cell inside me pushes me to move, to take her, knot her, stake my claim on her.

"It's now or never, Omega." I lean away from her and she reaches for me. Eyes half-dazed with desire, nostrils flaring, sweat shining on her skin.

She juts out her chin, "Fuck me, now."

Before she has completed the sentence, I thrust into her slick, wet channel and break through the barrier.

Her body bucks under me, and she flings her head back and screams.

The keening sound shimmers over my skin, tugs at my nerve endings.

The need in her voice is laced with a touch of desperation. Lust and fear roll off her in equal measure.

I want to ram into her again and again, but I stay where I am and let her adjust to my size.

My breath rasps out of me, and my heart hammers like I have been running for miles. I grit my teeth and stay unmoving, even as her moist pussy embraces my shaft.

She's so fucking tight and hot and wet.

Her body writhes and shudders; her nails dig into my biceps, rake over my back. Pain shudders down my spine and twines with the sheer pleasure of being inside her

I pull out again, all the way out.

I angle her hips up for better access and plow into her slickness with such force that her body moves up the bed and the frame slams against the wall.

Her body bucks, her hips wriggle under me, and her chest rises off the mattress.

A shudder rips through her.

A fresh spurt of moisture swirls out to greet my shaft.

I slam in all the way to the hilt. My knot engorges and following instinct, I hook my shaft behind her pelvic bone. Mine. Only mine. A fierce need coils in my chest and I thrust forward locking in as deep as I can.

Her pussy clamps around me, seducing me, giving me the pleasure of submission I so crave. Her spirit may deny it, but her body wants me, fucking needs me. Giving in, I let the hot streams of cum flood through her womb.

My hips clench, my groin tightens, and I know I am not done. I will not be done, not until I truly claim her.

Heat tugs at my nerve endings, the thought arousing me further. It shouldn't be possible, and yet I grow more hard. My balls feel too heavy and seem to drag me down.

Feeling my desire seems to affect her.

Her eyelids flutter open. Her pupils are dilated. The black of her pupils has completely taken over her irises, except for the pale, emerald-green ring around them. She swallows, looking at me completely dazed.

Fresh slick flows from inside her, tugging me, asking me to keep going.

I lower my mouth to her throat and sink my teeth into that soft skin at the curve of where her neck meets her shoulder.

# 12

Lucy

He bites the skin of my shoulder, and a flame of white heat arrows out to hurl through my veins, toward my chest. I scream out in pain even as a ball of heat throbs against my rib cage. I moan and thrash, but he doesn't let go.

The worst thing is that the pain clashes with my arousal and the mixture of the pain-pleasure only turns me on more. How is that possible?

I shouldn't be feeling the white-hot sting of arousal that guts me, that draws at a climax low in my belly.

His bulbous knot is locked inside me, and more hot streams of cum sear my womb.

I arch my legs up and hook them around him, digging my heels into his back. My spine curves off the bed; my chest thrusts out.

He grips my breast and squeezes a nipple. Another spurt of pain jolts down my spine.

Intense pleasure rolls over me, and the climax roars forward, then stops waiting for his touch, his hated…needed touch to make me come completely. "Please…" There's that word again. Why am I asking my tormentor for something my mind insists I don't want?

For something, my body insists that only he can give me? Only he can break this tearing need inside me. At this moment I loathe myself. That I was born an omega when all my life, all I've ever wanted was to be able to take, to fight for myself, for my clan…my family. The thought cleaves through the haze of need that has blinded me. Any moment now I'll tip over into the burning heart of the heat cycle and then I will no longer remember anything, not me, not him, not the goal I set out to achieve.

I need to do this while he's still inside me. While his knot pulses and my pussy clamps onto him and milks him. I need to do this if I want to see my fellow omegas go free.

With a last burst of clarity, I yank my hand still shackled in his grasp.

His grip loosens, and I slide my arm out.

I fling it to the side and reach blindly for something, anything I can use as a weapon… There, my fingers brush the lampshade on the side table.

I grab at it, but my sweaty fingers slide off it. I almost cry with frustration.

His muscles go solid, and his forehead crinkles. The desire in those glowering eyes is joined with a tinge of something else. Caution? And I almost regret doing this, almost. For a second, all I can think is damn them all, damn the world that always demands more than I am ready to give, my clan who always turn to me for protection… For with this man, the roles have reversed.

I can come into my omega self, I can allow myself to give up the part of me that caused so much strife and be what I am deep inside: a softer, more delicate, caring nurturer.

As if in agreement, my core pulses more moisture.

The heated walls of my womb clasp him hard, drawing out a fresh load of cum. The blue in his eyes recedes, and those eyes burn with a strange violet-tinged flame. It's fascinating. And I want him to always look at me that way. Then he raises his head, and blood gushes from the wound in my throat. The beast marked me… The horror of it sinks in. He claimed me… why would he do that? He could have rutted me and broken my heat cycle, but he went further.

His lips twist in a smirk.

My blood drips down his lips, down his chin to merge with the scarlet of his that bubbles from the wound where I had bitten him first. The ball of heat in my chest pulses.

I was wrong…we marked each other.

We claimed each other.

I am bonded to a stranger.

To someone, I don't know.

To only the biggest monster of all the land.

The one I came to kill, the one whose death will save my clan.

I raise the lamp and bring it down on his head.

# 13

Zeus

I sense her move, then the lamp smashes into the side of my head. Pain slices through my temples, and sparks of red flare behind my eyes. My hold on her loosens. But my knot inside her only strengthens. A fresh burst of desire slides into my blood, flowing all the way to the tip of my cock, engorging it further. Guess I should have told her that I have this propensity for violence... The harsher she is with me, the more it turns me on. I'll leave that information out for now. Just to see how far she'll go. How far can I hold out before my mind shuts down and the lust takes over? And what will that do to both of us?

I lower my head and purr, a long, low, angry purr that rips out from inside and folds over her.

Her gaze widens. The scent of her arousal intensifies. Her arm trembles and her grip on the lamp loosens.

I smash my head into the lamp and send it flying from her hands. It falls on the bed, then rolls to the floor and crashes. The sound doesn't penetrate the haze of the heat cycle that has her in its grasp.

Yanking her hand above her head, I wrap my fingers around both her delicate wrists. With my free hand, I reach down between us, scoop up some of our joined juices, my cum, her slick, a mixture that is pure aphrodisiac, and wipe her lips with it before shoving my finger inside her mouth.

Her lips curve around it, and she sucks on it. The feel of her lips on my skin dumps a wave of adrenaline into my blood; mixed with it is this primal need to finish what I started.

I move inside her, this time only with intent to punish. She mewls then cries out as I slam inside her all the way and let myself come again, coating her insides with hot, ropy streams of cum. Marking her inside and out.

"Mine," I growl.

Her eyelids fly open. Dark, fevered eyes stare back at me. The black of her pupils have completely taken over the green—the sign of an omega having completely submitted to her heat cycle. She bares her teeth.

I expect her to attack me again, or at the very least scream at me to get off of her, when, "More," she snarls and digs her heels into my back.

I freeze. Did I hear that correctly?

Her eyes narrow, then she raises her hips so I slide deeper inside—the swollen head of my cock brushes against her cervix.

She cries out, color draining from her cheeks. Her eyes plead with me. Her lips seduce me, and I can't stop myself. I take her lips and close my mouth over hers, fucking her with my tongue as much as my erect shaft penetrates her the way neither has ever pierced anyone else before.

The climax builds up from my groin, tightening, stretching, becoming big enough to overpower every part of me, plowing through me.

Her body shudders, and her teeth bite down on my lips as she falls apart.

I stay as I am, still half erect inside her.

She cracks her eyelids open and peers up at me.

I want to ask her why she tried to kill me—well, I know the answer why: she hates me. There's not much she can do about it, though. I claimed her as mine; she is my mate.

Her hips move of their own accord, her breath catches, and her lips turn downward. She rakes her nails down my biceps before clasping her fingers around my forearm.

I lean in and blow over her flushed face.

It's hot inside this room. Not only is it the height of summer, but I've nailed tight all the windows. I don't want the exterior of this city intruding and polluting the atmosphere inside.

Sweat drips down my chest. A drop plops on her breast, then another. Her gaze veers to my chest, to where my shaft is still locked inside her.

The sight arouses me again.

I move against her, and she croaks, a harsh sound. Her eyes fly open, and her gaze locks with mine. The dark of her irises deepens.

I am hurting her but also arousing her. And that pleases me immeasurably. The glow of satisfaction flushes my skin, and I don't question it. It doesn't matter to me that she gets as much pleasure from our coupling as I do. It doesn't.

I lean in and lick the bleeding wound on her shoulder.

She shudders, and a moan of pleasure is drawn from her.

I growl, a low, soothing purr, and her shoulders relax. Her thighs clench around my waist; the scent of slick deepens the air.

I want to hear her voice calling my name as she comes once again, as she rides my cock and her core shatters around me.

Still knotted inside her, I flip her over and above me.

# 14

Lucy

He flips me over so I am straddling him.

His knot is still heavy inside me, weighing me down, blocking all the cum that has streamed out of him.

The thought only makes me hotter. Desire ripples down my spine.

A low purr rumbles from his throat, stretching in the space between us. My stomach cramps, and I groan.

Inside me he grows bigger, and his knot flexes. Every part of me aches, and yet there is still this hunger. An emptiness that seems to grow bigger by the second, filling me, making me feel like I am searching, yearning for something more.

So much more. Of him. Of me. Of what he can do to me. Of what I want him to do to me. The force of my thoughts sends heat shooting through my blood. I bend down and hook my fingers in his hair, raking my nails down his scalp.

His shoulders flex. Red streaks his cheekbones. He growls again, but this time it has a tone of challenge laced through it.

His nostrils flare.

His gaze narrows.

He grips my waist and raises me, all the way up, until his shaft slips out and I stay poised right there with his knot blocking the entrance to my wet channel.

The feel of that roughened, ribbed skin against my soft inner walls sends a pulse of heat scrambling over my skin.

My toes curl; my thighs flex as I grip his waist. The feeling is so erotic, so much everything that starbursts of color flash behind my closed eyelids. I sway a little, and his grip firms on me.

"Look at me," he growls.

The command in his voice cuts through the intense feelings that have me in thrall.

I crack my eyelids open and meet his gaze—and hold on to that liquid blue in his eyes that seems to mirror back every last fragment of lust that I am feeling now.

It's as if he can read me, see through my soul, and I know I am being fanciful. Because he is an alpha who wants to show me that he is more superior, more dominant, yet my instinct says there is more, so much more to this man.

Right?

Wrong.

Was that why he'd dragged me here to his room and proceeded to bury his cock in me? His very large, very beautiful cock which he lowers me on again so the knot locks into place, holding me to him.

There's a low keening cry, and I realize it's me. I sound so aroused. So needy. Hungry for more. My chest pushes forward, my breasts thrusting out. I know my nipples are swollen, and my hair flows around me as I hold on to his forearms for balance.

The alpha is so damn massive, and the way he raises and lowers me again and again… And I am small, of course, in comparison. Still, the fact that he handles my body like I weigh nothing is both erotic and at the same time it makes me realize how much more powerful, how dominant he is.

A shudder of fear tugs at my nerves.

The still barely thinking part of my hindbrain, the one I've relied on to flag danger in all the time I'd been on the run from my homeland, sends a pulse of warning that creeps into my blood. It shoves away the sheer need that grips my body, that has pushed away all rational thought so far.

His hardness throbs inside me. Need radiates out from my core all the way to my toes.

And it feels so damn good.

I moan. Then shake my head, trying to clear it.

As if realizing that I am fighting the high of mating, and not wanting me to regain my composure, as if his very goal is to enfold me in the waves of pleasure which seize me, which roll down my spine, and make me hunch my back to try to keep in every last drop of moisture that is oozing out of me, he slides an arm up my back and grips the nape of my neck.

His touch sends a wave of intense desire surging through me. Sweat trickles down my throat, and my hair sticks to my forehead.

"Stop torturing me." I moan out the words, hear the pleading in them and refuse to let myself blush.

I am too far gone down this maze of pleasure in which he has me trapped.

My body is not my own anymore...it's an instrument of desire that he can tweak and play and tune to his heart's content.

He tugs me close so I am balanced above him, my breasts swinging right in front of his face.

"So fucking beautiful." His gaze rakes over my features—my lips, down to my chest. "I am going to give you so much pleasure you are going to forget everything: where you came from, what brought you here, your past, your present, everything except my name."

There's an authority in his voice that insists I agree with him. That I submit to the strength of his personality and give him what he wants. And it is precisely that which makes me straighten my spine. "You can't force me to do anything I don't want."

His gaze narrows, then his lips peel back in a smirk...which is not really a sign of amusement. Nope. It's a look so cruel, so full of the need to torment, so full of satisfaction that I blink. Not what I expected.

I'd thought he'd rage at me, perhaps turn me on my back and fuck me again. Instead, he gentles his hold on my neck and drags his palm over my skin, up into my hair.

His fingernails rake my scalp in a parody of what I'd done to him earlier. Goosebumps flare on my skin. The fine hairs on my forearms harden.

The difference between the intent I read on his features and the way he tailors his touch to seduce me, is so contradictory, that my head spins. My belly tightens, and to my horror, a fresh burst of slick gushes out to bathe his already swollen cock.

"You know exactly the right thing to do." His voice is soft.

His features compose into a look I cannot quite comprehend. His gaze is intense, brooding even, as if he's only now noticed me properly, realized I am not a submissive omega…and that's not what he wanted in the first place.

The realization sinks in.

This monster needs a challenge. He thrives on reaching for the unattainable. I've given him the perfect reason to redouble his efforts to mate me. To break me. He will not stop, not until he owns me completely, body and soul…not until he's ingrained his essence in every cell of my body.

The thought sends a wave of panic skittering over my skin.

At the same time his sheer confidence in how he thrusts his hips up so his massive shaft penetrates me, spears me, until it feels like I am being broken in half, is so completely arousing.

It feels like his very essence is reaching out to me, trying to overwhelm me, subsume me, and that's when the panic sets in.

I bite down on my lower lip.

Pain cleaves through the desire in my head. I bite the inside of my cheek, "Let me go."

One side of his lips curls and he takes his hands off of me, holding his arms up in front of me. In this moment I hate him more than anyone else I have ever hated before in my life.

He's doing this to prove a point. To show me that I am here of my own volition. That I don't have a choice but to be here impaled on his shaft. I push down on his chest, and the feel of those hard planes under my palms is so erotic, I don't realize I am sliding my palms in circles, cupping his skin, not until his gaze drops down to my hands, then back to my face.

"What have you decided, Omega?"

His voice is soft, confident.

His gaze holds mine steady.

Those irises of his are almost colorless. Gone is the passion that lurked in them earlier. Now they are considering, watching, stalking me. Waiting for me to move. He knows what I am going to decide, and I am helpless, caught in this trap he's woven around me.

Inside me, his shaft pulses. I gasp. My pussy clenches around the hard flesh. I squeeze my eyes shut to better absorb each ripple of desire that floods over my skin.

He's letting me go; he's giving me the perfect opportunity to tear myself off of him and stagger out. I push down with my knees into the mattress to do just that. But my body has other plans.

A tremor of heat flushes my skin; sweat breaks out on my brow and beads my upper lip. A spasm unfurls in my center and throbs out, asking, begging, needing this alpha to break my heat cycle.

I've only heard from the other omegas how agonizing it can be to see this through on your own. For during this very delicate time, your body is ready to receive, ready for the seed of an alpha to take root. Ready to be fucked and knotted, for that clawing, aching hollow inside to be filled with the engorged flesh. That shuddering, rasping friction that only comes with the thick, swollen alpha's member inside you, slamming through you, piercing you…as he is. Now.

"I hate you." The words sigh out of me, even as I slide up until my soft core catches on his bulbous knot, drawing a keening cry of delight from me. "Hate." I pant and lower myself around the knot. "You." The breath whistles out of me. The pleasure is so intense, I cannot stop myself from gripping his hair with renewed ferocity, holding on to him, pulling at the tufts, knowing I must be hurting him…and he deserves it. He deserves every last fraction of the pain that I am causing him, for not even that will make up for the anguish he's putting me through right now.

"You think you hate me." He slides one hand up my side to cup my breast, then positions the swollen flesh over his mouth. "But by the time I am done with you, you will no longer think so. No longer will you have the capacity to deny me…or yourself. For I intend to give you so much pleasure…so much pain, that it will wipe out everything that came before."

He closes his mouth around my swollen nipple and bites down. Not with so much force to hurt…and yet the surge of vibrations that rips through me, heads straight for my core, lighting up all my pleasure centres.

All my nerve endings seem to fire at once. The sensations arrow down to collect right there around my already engorged clit. It's too much. Too soon. Yet not enough. I pant and strain against him. Needing, wanting, what? What do I want?

He lowers his head, and his gaze locks on me. He waits, every part of his body tense, his muscles shuddering, watching me, stalking me, holding out for something more from me. I swallow and wait. Wait. My chest heaves and sweat beads my forehead.

He slides his palm between our bodies and grinds the heel against my clit. Red and white sparks flash behind my eyes and I cry out. My hips jerk, slick gushes from my channel, and my inner muscles clamp down on his throbbing dick.

His eyes flare and his shaft thickens even more inside of me, the knot widening until it seems to fill me completely. With a harsh growl he lunges forward, going impossibly deep inside of me. My body bucks; every muscle in my pussy quivers. The climax rips up from my toes and then sweeps up my thighs, arches my spine, bouncing over my skin, vibrating up my throat, and I scream as I come.

He peels back his lips, and with a last thrust, locks into place behind my pelvic bone. His muscles ripple and with a triumphant roar he shoots hot jets of cum into my womb.

My eardrums pop, and then there is complete silence.

A velvety white, so soothing that I know it cannot possibly be real, flows over me, cocooning me, and I let it drag me down.

# 15

Zeus

Her body goes limp, and she falls over.

I guide her down to lay on me. Her shoulders twitch, and then her muscles relax as sleep takes over.

Sprawled across my chest, her head fits under my chin. Her breathing is deep, like one who has been spent.

It satisfies me to know that my omega is content, for now.

There are things I want to do to her which I've never wanted to do to anyone else, and that in itself is a shock.

Since she'd walked into my space and I had taken a whiff of her scent, I'd known she was mine.

Call it primitive, but it is the wont of the alpha to dominate, and any omega chosen by me had better be grateful I am going to see her through her heat cycle.

I tighten my arms around her, and she moans. It's such an inherently feminine sound, so completely contradictory to everything I am, that I harden again.

She burrows in deeper, and warmth floods my chest.

I unhook one arm from around her. Reaching up I brush my fingers over her mark at the side of my throat.

No one has done that before.

Not even the more uncontrollable alpha females who I have on occasion taken to bed. And only for the satisfaction of bending them to my will before allowing them to find release. As for the omegas? Most had been too tame, too ready to spread their legs so I could rut them to release.

This wildling is unlike any female I've met. She'd gone straight for the jugular, literally speaking. And it doesn't bother me as much as it should. And it should really. It should worry me very much that this little slip of a not-very-submissive omega swept in and seduced me with her cunt, her heat, her scent. She could distract me from the plans I'd worked on for so long. A skitter of apprehension tugs my nerves.

I am so close to taking over the Scots and becoming far more powerful than Golan ever was. Nothing and no one can sway me from my goal. She's a pleasant distraction, no more. My very own plaything, who will do as I bid her. I'll seduce her, make her so hungry for my touch, for every shred of my affection, that she'll beg me for satisfaction.

I will shield her from the world, and in return, she'll provide me with many moments of pleasure. She's a means to forget where I came from, a relief from the responsibilities that lie in store for me, for even the alpha at the top of the food chain, aka me, needs an omega to satisfy him.

While she marked me first, it is the alpha's claim that matters. I forged the mating bond with her and took her as my mate. And she'd better be grateful for that.

I rub my cheek against her hair. "Wake up, sweetheart, your true mate is here."

# 16

Lucy

His voice whispers in my ear. Seductive, beautiful, it shivers over my nerve endings. The heat of his body cocoons me. I feel safe and secure. And that can't be right. A flicker, a hum of contentment rolls out of me. I rub my cheek against the hard, unforgiving planes of his chest. He curves his body around me, and it feels so right.

Is this what it feels like to be home? But I don't have a home. Not since my country was invaded, and my father made a deal with the Vikings—virgin omegas for the life of his people.

I'd managed to escape with as many of the omega women as I could save.

We'd stowed away on a ship to Scotland, and the leader of the Scots had agreed to protect us. On one condition. I had to comply with his plan of sneaking into the General's stronghold and killing him.

I had failed in my mission.

Now I was going to meet the fate of almost every omega captured by an alpha. I was going to be mated and I am sure, eventually, bred. Only omegas can give birth. In these times of declining population, it should have been a blessing to be born one. Why, then, has it always felt like a curse?

He yanks my hair back, and heat prickles over my scalp. It doesn't hurt not exactly...more of that pleasure-pain I am coming to associate with him.

I moan and force my eyes open, knowing already what I am going to see. That I am trapped, under the watchful gaze of my mate.

My monster.

Chills rack my body, immediately chased by heat. It rises from my belly, bubbling up to the cord that is curled against my breast bone. The heavy coil that binds me to him.

A hum of betrayal tightens my chest.

He is the strongest alpha in the land, yet he's also the General, the ruler of this country.

Will he listen to me if I explain why I broke into his stronghold?

As if sensing my emotions and realizing that my rational self is asserting itself despite the heat cycle in which I am still trapped, he flips me over. I am on my back, and his big hulking figure is bent over me. He's all around me, and I should feel what? Threatened? Afraid? But I am not. And that scares me further.

It also arouses me.

All other thought spills from my head. I cannot think about the world outside, about the other omegas who wait for news from me.

"Do it," I narrow my eyes.

His arousal throbs.

His lips curl in a smirk, then he pulls out of me. The knot has lessened and he slips out with very little pain. Had he waited until now so he didn't hurt me? If so, why didn't he let go of me earlier? Why has he held me on his chest, his fingers running over the back of my hair, my spine? Goose-bumps flare on my skin. Had he taken care of me? No, I don't want that. I want him to be exactly what the role demands of him. An alpha. Who takes and rapes and pillages?

He didn't rape me, though, did he?

He'd waited and seduced until I'd asked him to fuck me.

My face heats at the memory.

I hadn't wanted him, and yet my body had given in and been a willing participant in how he'd taken me.

My shoulders tense at the thought, and a whimper of protest coils up my throat. I don't stop it; I couldn't if I wanted to. Without him inside me, that emptiness crawls in on itself. It aches. I ache.

Every part of my skin feels like it is being stretched.

Heat flushes my skin. Sweat drenches my back. My lips are dry, so dry. And yet between my legs a fresh dose of slick trickles down.

His nostrils flare, and a low purr grumbles up his massive chest. It only sinks into my skin, rolls over that damned throbbing in my chest, and twines with it.

It hurts me and yet it also feels right.

It doesn't make any sense.

Nothing makes sense. Except the animal on top of me, who'd rutted me not a few minutes ago. Of whom I want more.

I raise my chin and lick my lips. My hips arch of their own accord so my melting core brushes against his already hardening cock.

His gaze narrows; silver sparks flare in those blue eyes. His lips pull back in a snarl. And I am almost relieved. This I know, this creature born of need, of hunger, trying to fulfill the most basic of desires, hunger, sex, thirst...these urges I can manage. I don't want to think beyond that, not now.

He slides down my body, and as if knowing exactly what I had thought, what I had wanted, he grabs my thighs and shoves them apart. Sliding his big palm under my hips, he holds me up and fits his lips to my core.

My eyes roll back, and my mouth opens in a silent scream, only his hand glides up, and he shoves his thumb between my lips. I don't question it. I bite down around his digit, to anchor myself.

His tongue is inside my pussy, licking me, sucking me. A growl rumbles up from him and draws forth a fresh stream of slick. He licks it up, swallows it, then comes back for more.

He fastens his teeth around the bud of my clit, and stars explode behind my closed eyelids.

He still doesn't let me go.

My fingers are wrapped in his hair, trying to pull him away, trying to hold him close.

My thighs are wound around his head, and I am half off the mattress, and all I can think is: fuck, more. I want more.

Then he drags his other thumb down my butt and toward the puckered hole between my ass cheeks. I freeze. My eyes fly open. But he's a step ahead of me. His finger slips into my wet, streaming channel, scoops up my slick, and spreads it around my back hole.

He traces the puckered ring of the hole, and a shiver runs up my spine.

He thrusts his tongue into my pussy, then with the heel of his hand he rubs my clit.

His finger slips into the hole.

The combination of his tongue inside me, his thumb in my mouth, and the finger in my back hole is too much.

The climax crashes over me. I scream and bite down on his thumb; my back arches up and off the bed. Before I can collapse, he flips me, yanks up my hips, and enters my wet channel from behind.

# 17

Zeus

I'd meant to take her, put her in her place, show her that she is an omega who has to submit to me. I'd meant to be harsh, not caring for her needs. And I wasn't. I was only satisfying myself. If, during that time, I also gave her pleasure, well, what is the harm in that?

As it is, I can't get enough of her body, her soft skin, her warm, tight pussy that clasps around me.

The still rational part of my brain twinges, and I push it away.

I shove aside all thought, everything except for the desire that tightens my groin. The blood that rushes to my shaft, thickening its head so it flares up and knots into place. I am going to make sure that none of my fluid slips out. Make sure every part of my hardness is sheathed inside her. Under me, she thrashes her head from side to side. Her back arches off the bed and slams into me. Her arms push down on the mattress, shoving the curve of her spine into my chest.

I am bent over her, covering her with my much bigger self, protecting her... I clamp down on that emotion. Nothing, I am allowed to feel nothing for her, remember?

Nothing except this greedy need to take...to give, to bring her to climax again and again, to make he take every last bit of my cum as I gush into her, jetting the very essence of what I am right inside her, hitting her womb.

I cry out, and then for a second time, I bite down on her shoulder, right over where I'd marked her the first time. This time it's a true mating, one in the heat of passion, one without any ulterior motive, one meant to solidify my claim on her. She throws her head back and screams, and the sound bounces around the room and slams over me, and it feels right. I taste her blood and draw back, licking the puncture marks, trying to soothe her, to deaden some of the pain. I shouldn't be doing it, but I can't help myself anymore.

Everything in my past has already vanished. All I am is an alpha, and she is my omega.

My mate.

That's all that matters.

I lower her, even as I turn her on her side and keep her wrapped in my arms. I purr, letting the vibrations of my chest resonate against her back. She moans in her throat, rubs her cheek where it is pillowed on my biceps. I let her draw comfort from me.

I want to deny it.

I should deny it.

But I can't. And I am too content, too replete to not give in to the need to comfort her either.

I wrap my other arm around her waist and draw her close. I'm flaccid now, the knot having diminished in size so that I can pull out of her, but I don't. I stay right there. After all, she is mine, isn't she?

Over the next two days I manage to persuade her to eat at regular intervals. It's not altruistic of me to do so, nor is it that I am worried about her in any way. Nope, it's purely selfish, honest. I want to keep her energy up, so she can be an active participant in our mating. I need her to be conscious, to feel every ridge of my engorged dick when I bury myself balls deep in her; as I bring her to climax and knot her over and over again. And the feral thing that she is, she takes from me, matches me move for move, until finally sated and stripped of all defense, she curls up at my side and falls into exhausted slumber.

I throw my thigh over her hip to hold her captive, then close my eyes.

A loud banging echoes through the room. I grab my omega and pull her close, wanting to shield her from whoever is behind the door.

"Who the fuck is there?" I crack my eyelids open.

Her body shudders in my arms. Her gaze is bewildered, her lips swollen, the claiming mark at the base of her neck still bleeding. Every part of her has been marked, ravaged, taken. She is caked in my cum, and it's so glorious. I don't stop myself from throwing back my head and shouting my exultation. That pure animal feeling of satisfaction that comes from having rutted so thoroughly.

When I look down, I expect to see her cowering against the pillows, perhaps curled up and crying. Instead, she's watching me with an intent gaze as if she's trying to understand what I am feeling right now.

It feels so right...that I know it's wrong.

There's another loud knocking on the door.

"I don't mean to coitus interruptus," Ethan's voice filters through, "but you'd never forgive me if I didn't remind you about the meeting of the Council that you called for to discuss the situation with the Scots?"

Right. Meeting. About the Scots. I should have pushed it back, but I hadn't been in my right mind when I'd barged in here with the omega. I'd expected to have stayed for a few hours... normally that's all it's taken for me to have broken an omega's heat cycle in the past.

"You've been in there for a straight seventy-two hours, General," Ethan helpfully informs me again.

The fucker is probably gloating at how the mighty Zeus lost all track of time buried in his omega's sweet pussy.

Not any omega. I'd been wrapped up in my mate for three days. Which is understandable, even for a bastard like me. It takes months to consolidate a mating bond. I could be forgiven a few days. Not. Nothing comes between me and my plans to take over the Scots.

I square my shoulders. A better man would explain to her why it is important that I have to leave, and that I won't take too long. That I'll be back before she has a chance to fret and miss me.

She pushes at me, and I loosen my arms from around her. She moves away and her breasts sway. The rounded flesh is reddened from my ministrations. Her dark-pink nipples swell under my gaze. A shudder of heat tightens my gut. Perhaps I should stay with her, bring her down from the high of the mating before I leave. Yeah, a considerate alpha would do that. Which I am not.

"How long do your heat cycles last?"

She swallows then, some more of the haze from her eyes clearing, and it makes me want to cover her body with mine and fuck her all over again, until that dazed, dilated look is permanently etched in her eyes. The sheer primal need of it thickens my shaft which is still inside her.

As if sensing my need, a fresh stream of slick shivers down her thigh.

"Answer me." I'd wanted to be curt, but the words had come out almost soft.

"Three." She shakes her head as if to clear it. "Perhaps four days."

So she's almost at the end of her heat cycle. A surge of something suspiciously like relief lightens my chest. Nope, that can't be right.

Why should it matter to me that she should be able to cope fine when I leave her? Why does a part of me want her to miss me? And the fact that when I return, she'll still be here waiting for me? I need to hurry and get the meeting over with.

I really should leave right now.

She shifts in my arms. Her hair flows over her shoulder, and I can't stop myself winding it around my palm.

She bites her lip.

I bury my nose in her neck and draw in that sweet, sugary scent of hers, laced with that deeper, spicier tang of me.

The bond in my chest writhes. I stiffen. The mating bond. I rub the skin over my heart, trying to settle the restless ball of heat lurking under my ribcage.

I'd known what I was doing when I'd marked her.

Had decided as soon as I'd set eyes on her that I was going to claim her, so why does this reminder of what she is confuse me?

Why do I want to hold her close and explain why I must leave her, just for a little while?

I pull out of her and my dick slides out with a wet plop. Liquid gushes out of her pussy and sloshes down her inner thigh. My cum. Her juices. The interlaced scent of our joined arousal reeks into the air.

A pulse springs to life at my temples, in my balls, even at the back of my eyelids. Fuck me. What is this omega doing to me?

She gasps and my skin tightens, a jolt of unease crawls down my spine. How am I already so tuned into her? Fuck this. I need to walk away from her, show her she has no influence over me.

I swing my legs over the side.

Rising to my feet, I stalk away from the bed to where I'd disposed of my clothes and slide them on.

Dense clouds of tension roll off her, and I feel her uncertainty tug at me through the bond. She doesn't say anything. Had I been expecting her to call out to me?

To stop me?

Perhaps ask me to take her again? She doesn't, and something like disappointment weighs me down. I pull my boots on, then walk out of there.

# 18

Lucy

I am not sure how long I snoozed for, but the sound of the door opening sweeps through my subconscious mind. I stir and wake up, wondering where I am. The ceiling above is unfamiliar, the bed below me too smooth, too soft. I shudder and take in a breath of air and find it is scented with his fragrance. The beast has left, but his musk is everywhere, on me, in the room.

I turn and crack my eyelids open. My eyelashes are caked. I wipe away whatever is clogging them, knowing it is a mixture of sweat and his cum and our fluids, the fluids he'd dribbled into my mouth that I had swallowed down like it was the last drop of moisture I'd find in the world. The memory of how I'd given myself to him and asked him to take me, all of it crowds in on me.

My body shudders in remembrance of his touch. Slick gathers between my legs. There's movement in the room, and I know I must sit up, but I can't. I groan, and my voice comes out all wrong. I can barely swallow.

I need water.

My tongue is so dry it feels swollen and fills my mouth, along with his taste. The salty taste of his skin, the sweet musk of his essence, the sugary, tangy mixture of both fluids…all of it pops goosebumps on my skin. I push myself up against the pillows only to find that every part of me aches. Through half-closed eyes, I see a woman place fresh food and water on the table.

She doesn't look at me, keeps her eyes averted. "The General has commanded that you eat and drink before he returns."

"Who are you?" I try to say the words out loud, but of course, nothing emerges.

Before I can repeat myself, she turns and leaves. The door shuts behind her with a soft snick. Whispered words filter through, then the bolts drop into place. I am alone once more. And truth be told, I am relieved. I wouldn't want anyone else to witness how far I have fallen. That I am here wallowing in the outcome of my mating still in the last throes of my heat cycle, floating in and out. I'd let the General break my cycle and stake his claim on me.

I hadn't resisted enough.

Yet a part of me insists there is nothing I could have done. I am an omega, and this was bound to happen. He'd taken me so many times I'd lost count. Soon he is going to be back and no doubt he is going to fuck me many times more. A shudder of heat flushes my skin, and my guts twist with apprehension.

I have to resist him.

I must push back. It'll only make things more difficult for me. But that's fine. I've come this far; I've infiltrated the General's stronghold. Now all I have to do is wait for the opportune moment and try to kill him again. Once that is done, I can return to Kayden, and he will free my clan. My stomach twists. With grief…with hunger.

The scent of food teases my nostrils.

But I shouldn't eat. I shouldn't.

I am here being fed, so I can get energy back, no doubt for another mating, while the other omegas must be eagerly waiting for news of my mission.

I need to complete my mission and rescue them.

Straightening my spine, I swing my legs over the side of the bed and stand. My knees almost buckle. My thigh muscles scream in protest. My left shoulder throbs. A fresh surge of blood drips down my throat. I hold my palm to the wound where he marked me, the wound I don't want to acknowledge, but the throbbing in my chest responds to the ache.

It's as if the cord that binds me to that monster recognizes its master.

My body may crave him, may want him, may even acknowledge his dominance, but not my soul. Not my mind. Not my emotions. I know I can hold out on him. When I am not in heat, when I am more myself…when.

The scent of food grows stronger. Sometime in the last few minutes I've crossed the floor to the table in my confused state and now I stand in front of the table bearing the tray. I should eat it. I shouldn't. I can't. I must. To keep up my strength. To keep myself together. Just until I find a way to kill the monster.

I had been wrong to approach Kayden and agree to his plan. I'd foolishly thought I had a chance. Truth is, I hadn't been thinking straight. I'd gone with what my instinct said was right. And look where that landed me.

Imprisoned in the den of the monster, in the middle of a heat cycle which twists my guts. Sweat breaks out on my skin and my womb clenches in need. My teeth chatter, my toes dig into the floor. I am hot and cold all at once. Not good, this is not good. I am going into the home stretch of the heat cycle. The last day is always the worst.

Why isn't that alpha-hole here when I need him, when I want him to take me and rut me and shove away the pain that taints my insides?

Moaning, I wrap my arm around my middle and reach for the plate, only for it to crash to the floor.

I cry out in anger, in fear, in shame, then drop to my knees, curling up on my side in front of it.

# 19

Zeus

I stride down the corridor without cleaning myself up. Perhaps I should have showered, but the fact is that I want her scent on me.

I want to show her claiming mark and I am still unsure why. It isn't that common for omegas to mark their alphas. Rarer still for alphas to flaunt them. But I want to do so.

A sign to them she is mine and off limits to anyone else. She is my mate, the one I chose…the one who chose me.

Or maybe it's just this primal need inside me to make sure they can smell her on me, feel my satisfaction and know that she waits for me back in my suite.

Not that any of them would dare to touch her, and if anyone dares look at her, I'll burn out their eyes, I'll gut them… I'll—

A touch on my shoulder snaps me out of my thoughts.

"She's in your head." I look around to find Ethan standing at my shoulder. His features are calm, his gaze wary.

When I had killed my father and taken his place, Ethan had been the first to pledge his loyalty to me. It still didn't change the fact that he came from the ruling classes. The same as the alphas who had misused their power and hastened my mother's death.

"Second." I stalk to the head of the table.

Ethan drops into the chair on my right.

I glower at the assembled men. "When do we attack Scotland?"

My gaze sweeps the room.

There's silence, then Solomon leans forward. "It's not a good idea, General."

I train my gaze on Sol. "Is that right?" My voice is low and measured.

Solomon pales under his tan.

I'd hand picked him to become my Head of Troops. Not that it matters. As long as he follows my lead, I'll be tolerant of him.

"Answer me." My voice rings through the room.

Sol's gaze flicks to Ethan.

"The timing is not yet right to take on the Scots." He swallows, then squares his shoulders. "We need to arm the soldiers and train the new recruits. Also need to source more weapons. It's premature to attack."

"All of you agree?" I look around the table.

"We are not yet prepared," Liam growls.

"Care to elaborate?" I thrust out my chest. It's a subtle act of dominance, warning off the other man, telling him that I am stronger, more powerful than him, and not just physically.

"I am the first to want to wipe out the Scots for their slaughtering my family, but I know the importance of not rushing in." The tank of an alpha pounds his fist on the table for emphasis. "When we finally attack, I want to do so with all our might. Kill them in one go."

Well, at least he speaks his mind.

"Anyone else?"

"Since we are all in such a chummy mood," Ryker drawls from the other side of the table, "perhaps you need to spend time consummating your bond with your omega, get it all out of your system so you are not distracted when we fight the Scots."

Anger bubbles up, the emotions ripe and thick and coiling through my blood. I taste the need for violence on my tongue, so rich, so strong. "Is that what you'd do if you were in my place?"

Ryker's shoulders stiffen. He's one hell of a marksman, the best on my team. Doesn't mean I have to spare him. No one is indispensable, and he knows it. He swallows, then nods.

"You're right." I let my lips twist in the semblance of a smirk.

A breath rushes out of Ryker; his shoulders visibly relax.

"That's the last time I tolerate anyone talking about my omega. No-one is to even glance at her, got it?"

Silence.

I glower around the table, making sure to look each alpha in the eye.

Ryker gets to his feet. "That's our cue then." He glides out of the room. Sol and the other alphas follow.

Well, all except Ethan who stays seated. He brings his fingers together in front of him. A nerve tics at his temple. He sets his jaw. Adamant fucker. He will not leave without having his say, and the frustrating thing is that I am going to let him do just that, too. Fuck! Leaning forward, I brush the dust off his shoulder. "What?"

He doesn't get the threat inherent in my gesture, or if he does, he chooses to ignore it. Fucker has some balls.

"You count on me to tell the truth." He holds my gaze.

He's right, and fuck if that doesn't infuriate me. Anger heats my blood. "I keep you because you had no other place to go."

"And isn't that a fact." Ethan lowers his palms and drums his fingers on the table. "I was born here; these are my people, and I plan to do my best by them."

"Your misplaced sense of loyalty will bite you in the ass," I glower.

"Your trying to hide what you always feel whether it is to your men or to your omega will—"

Only when I feel the rough cloth of Ethan's collar under my fingers do I realize I've closed the space and hauled the slimmer man up to his toes. "I warned you not to talk about her," I snarl.

"And if I obeyed you every single time you issued a command, I'd be mistaken for a beta." Ethan's lips twist.

Annoyingly, he is right again.

Sure, I have an ego, but I also know I don't want to surround myself with men who agree to everything I say. That's what Golan did, and look what happened to him. A harsh chuckle rolls out of me. "Speak then." I let go of him.

He crashes into the table, then rights himself. "You should have sent the omega to the harem." He pauses as if choosing his words with care.

Ethan thinks things through down to the last detail before he takes action. Me? I lead with my gut.

"Go on." The mating cord nestled under my breastbone throbs. A shudder of awareness rolls down my spine, twining with something else, a faint sense of unease. I rub the skin of my chest above my heart.

"It's the deal you made with us." Ethan sets his jaw. "No alpha is allowed to touch omegas without their permission. How do you expect your men to live by your code when you can't follow it yourself?"

The blood thuds at my temples, my left eyebrow throbs. "I wanted her; I took her." I lean forward and shove my face close to his. "No one comes near her, until I decide what to do with her."

His lips tighten. His entire demeanor is one of censure. And I thought when I'd killed off Golan, I'd gotten rid of the ghost of parental disapproval. Fuck this. I don't owe an explanation to anyone.

"I don't march to anyone else's tune or follow anyone else's timetable, only my own." I grind my jaw so hard that pain slashes down my throat. "We will attack Scotland and bring Kayden to his knees."

"We need more time—"

I raise my hand, cutting him off. "We will wait a few more days… Until I have made sure my omega is settled. Then we attack." I turn to leave.

"We chose you for our leader, Zeus. The underbelly of this city needs to be swept clean of the criminals and the corruption fostered under your father's rule. You are the only man who can show us the way."

I pause halfway to the door. A cold feeling rolls in my gut.

He is wrong, so wrong. I'm just the bastard from the wrong side of the tracks who is always on the outside looking in. I believe in only one thing: fighting for myself, for my survival. That is it. Nothing else matters. Not this city. Not the people. Not my Council. Nothing.

I glare at him over my shoulder. "Don't patronize me." My voice is deceptively light. Blood thuds at my temples. "Do. You. Understand?"

Ethan's jaw hardens, then he lowers his gaze. "General."

I should feel some satisfaction that the other man has submitted, has acknowledged my superiority.

Yet it only leaves a feeling of distaste in my mouth.

The mating bond shudders and pushes up against my chest. Dense waves of fear bleed from the cord. My gut churns.

The omega...she is restless and afraid. She needs me. I stride to the exit and shove the doors open.

## 20

Lucy

The pain shudders over my skin. My shoulders jerk, and my chest thrusts up and off the floor.

My stomach twists, and I taste the acidic tang of bile. I want to scream, but all that emerges is a whimper.

I moan and curl in on myself.

There is this hunger gnawing at me. It churns at my guts, growing bigger by the second, as if it's going to tear open my skin and rip out of me at any time. I am hungry, so hungry. And it's not for food. I want him… need him…to fill me. To shove aside this hollowness that's drawing me in, threatening to overwhelm me.

I want him throbbing inside me. The thought is so intense I almost imagine he is here, his massive body bent over me, his hard thighs pushing my legs apart, then him slamming into me, burying his brutal length in me, holding me down, folding his body around me, protecting me, taking me, cherishing me. The thought sends heat shooting through my veins. Sweat beads my brow.

My chest heaves.

My breasts ache.

Every part of me screams and begs for his touch.

I want to call out to him. I need to call out to him. The urge is so overwhelming that I feel every last coherent thought trickle out of me, leaving only the pure essence of the omega I am behind.

To be a receiver, to take, the breeder.

Isn't that what my mother told me? And I had resisted it every step of the way. At least my father, for the short time he'd been around, had encouraged me to fight the urge.

He'd been the rare male alpha who'd actually not conformed to the stereotype. Who'd seemed to understand what it means to live a life where you are constantly living from one heat cycle to the other. Fighting it each time. Terrified of that hunger that sweeps in with the onset of each mating loop. Worried that this cycle is the one where you give in and seek out an alpha to break the cycle and put an end to the suffering. It was one-sided. So unjust. Nature had decreed that with the plummeting population count, omegas in the heat cycle would attract every single alpha in the square mile around them. Send enough into the rut that they would seek you out and try to take you.

Most of my omega friends had rejoiced with the onset of their cycles. Dreaming of the alpha who they would choose as their mate. Not me. I wanted to hold on to my independence for as long as I could. No alpha-hole male is going to break me. No, I am my own person and intend to be this way for as long as I can. I had opted to take fertilization blockers — fringe benefits of being royalty? I had the means to purchase the drugs from the black market — and subdue my hormones. I'd pushed my heat cycles further and further apart, and been able to spar with alphas without attracting their attention.

I thought it was working…until I had sensed him and my true nature had come roaring out.

Another white-hot cycle of pain rips through me and catches in my throat. I don't have the energy to scream to try to relieve some of that burning pressure.

My womb cramps, and the fluid begs to be secreted.

All it needs is an alpha's purr, his scent to draw it out and satisfy this hunger that demands his touch. Where the hell is he when I need him? I bang the side of my head against the floor in the hope of relieving some of the pain, or at least to hurt some other part of me so as to distract me from the core source of pain. Inside me.

Deep inside me.

In the very center of my being.

The sound of footsteps grows closer. Am I imagining it? A faint rumble of voices, then the air from the corridor flows over my flushed forehead, then the door slams shut.

I scent him first.

That spice of burned pinewood seeps through the air. My mouth waters. Or maybe it's just that I am thirsty?

The pace of the footsteps increases, then I feel him kneel down next to me.

I expect him to berate me, to perhaps hit me for messing up his space or maybe slide me on my back and take me…which is what I want, damn it!

Tears prick the backs of my closed eyelids, and I let them trickle down my cheeks.

I couldn't stop it if I wanted to.

I want him to fuck me, to take me mercilessly and put an end to the dense, cloying pain that thuds through my guts, that fills my head, pounds at my temples. I just want it gone.

I open my mouth to ask him to do just that, while a part of me cringes at the shame of it. This is my sworn enemy—he'd taken me against my will, and now I want him to do it again. And again.

I try to move my limbs but only manage a slight jerk of my hands.

He seems to understand, though, for his arms come around me and scoop me up.

Every muscle in my body tenses.

I am sure he is going to fuck me when I am at my weakest.

When I need him the most. When I don't really want him, but my body is not going to cooperate with my will.

I want…to get the hell out of here.

I want...to turn back time to when I'd met Kayden, and tell him I do not agree to his plan.

I want...the feel of the alpha's arms around me, cradling me closer, his lips sliding over my fevered forehead as he walks into the bathroom holding me.

The sound of running water fills the space. It splashes over my face and I gasp. It's cold. Too cold. Goosebumps pop on my skin. My shoulders quiver. I gulp, and the breath catches in my throat. I open my mouth, and water slides in. I gurgle and shove at the wall of muscle at my back.

"Shh."

Has he actually placed his chin on my head? Is he actually being this gentle with me? I feel the purr vibrate up his chest as he holds me flush against him. Instantly, my muscles unwind.

My shoulders shudder.

It feels like every part of me is reacting to him, tuning in to him. Drawing in every last cadence of that purr that rolls over me, sinks into my blood, uncoiling that tension that grips my flesh.

My shoulders slump, my knees go weak, and I would have fallen, except his arm is around my waist, propping me up.

The water is no longer cold.

It seems to hit my fevered skin and to absorb some of the heat before it flows away. The throbbing in my forehead dulls.

All through it, he keeps purring— a low, deep, comforting sound that coils around me, soothing away more of my aches, trembling down my spine, down the backs of my thighs.

I am floating; my limbs feel so heavy. My eyelids feel like they are weighed down. I should protest and tell him he can't manipulate my body like this. He has no right.

My muscles tense again.

My hands twitch as I try to raise them. I fold my other arm above my chest, place my mouth next to his ear, and allow another husky purr to wind around me.

He pulls me back against that solid wall of his chest. My head rolls back, and I let sleep pull me down.

When I awake next the room is dark.

I feel the soft sheets under my cheek; something silken covers me. My insides twist, but this time it is something else…a different kind of hunger. My limbs feel too weak, but I force myself to open my eyes.

A shape moves in the dark next to me.

I scream and spring up.

# 21

Zeus

She screams, and the noise rips through my guts. It shouldn't affect me. She is just someone I had decided to take for my own and keep on a whim...except that's not true, not anymore. Fact is, from the moment I had seen her, scented her, laid eyes on her, there was a powerful pull toward her. One I can't yet understand.

Except I need her with me, need to bury myself in her softness and slake my hunger.

To satisfy her while I am at it, too. Why is it so important that I soothe her? I don't want to go to her and yet I cannot help myself. I am not aware that I am on my feet and moving to her, not until I am sitting next to her on the bed. Not until she's flung herself at me, tearing at me with her nails. She growls, and there are tears dripping down her cheeks as she flings herself at me again and again. Pain comes off her in waves. And terror, the sheer terror of the unknown. Mixed with it is the whiff of hunger. A need so powerful that a growl rumbles up my chest. It's torn out of me, flowing through the air. My very insides seem to be begging me to stop her, take her close, protect her. I curl my fingers into fists at my sides, digging my nails into my flesh. Pain shudders up my arms, but I push it aside. All my attention is taken up by the tiny thing who is trying to climb me, who is crawling up my chest, to wrap her arms and legs around me.

"Please." She clings to me.

Her voice breaks.

I need to bring her closer, take her to me, draw her essence inside me... and yet I resist. I am not sure why. Is it because the way she suffers satisfies some deep-rooted hunger inside? The need to rut, to kill, which has been with me from the very start, from the time I saw my father hurt my mother, over and over again as he tried to take her, make her bend to his will? And my mother had resisted every step of the way. Until the bastard had broken her physically, and yet her spirit hadn't given in. She'd resisted.

Like she is. My little omega who bares her teeth at me.

"Why are you not taking me, fucking me as a red-blooded alpha should?"

"Is that what you want?"

My voice comes out harsh, and I don't recognize it. It sounds like a man at the edge of despair, an alpha at the edge of his control. And I have been holding on to the shreds of that ever-weakening control of mine. I hadn't been aware of that, not until now.

Not until she snarls, "I demand that you fuck me and take my pain away. That you break me and find that part inside of me that wants to be revealed to the world. I ask that you then feed me, for I am hungry. Hungry. Do you understand, Alpha?"

The crudeness of her words sends a keening cry of desire rippling down my spine. My cock hardens. My groin throbs. "You are not in your senses; you don't know what you are asking—"

She grabs the back of my hair and yanks me close with such force that my head snaps forward.

"How do you know what I want? How can you possibly know the depth of hunger that twists my insides, that bubbles up from my very womb, that yearns for your touch, your heat to fill me, that needs your seed to soothe it, to fulfill it? To take root. How can you know the depth of want that drives me to open my eyes, my mouth, my soul and ask for you to take me? Even as the part of me that is rational and independent that was taught to fend for myself and survive without an alpha cringes and wails at the depths to which I have fallen?"

She pants to a stop, chest heaving, red lips glistening. The scent of her need fills the space, crashing over me.

I lean in until our noses bump, until I can see the pores on her cheek, the flush that stains her skin, the freckles that dot the creamy expanse of her breasts. "Once I start there is no going back." I want to smirk, to pretend it's a joke, to show her that I am the dangerous one in this relationship—and I am, of course I am.

For I am bigger, more physically powerful, much stronger than her.

And yet, as she raises herself on her knees so her eyes are level with mine, so the heat of her core flows over my chest, I know she packs a powerful punch, too. Perhaps we are more equally matched than we realize. Perhaps that is why the force in me that needs to take, relishes the challenge. For that's what she is. A challenge. Prey. One I can toy with, play with, without fear. For she will not break, not that easily.

And I will keep trying over and over again, so she gives a little every time.

And when she finally goes over the edge, I'll be there to taste my spoils.

Her complete submission, it will be so beautiful.

So erotic.

A thing of pleasure that will be well worth the effort. And break she will.

I intend to take every single part of her until she is pleading with me to stop.

Until she is begging for more.

Until her very spirit cries out for me.

Until I own her. Absolutely.

The thought of it is such a turn-on that desire hardens my groin. My cock strains against my pants, its need twisting my insides. While every part of me readies to take her, to bend her to my will.

"Promises, promises, Alpha. Are you going to just sit there talking or are you going to live up to your words?"

Anger brushes my nerves. My skin tightens with the overwhelming need to take, to possess, to consume. "Don't provoke me, Omega."

I shove her away, not gently. "Not unless you can take the consequences of your actions." I am past any pretense. She wants to see what I am. She wants to feel the monster inside. The one who is insatiable, who will not stop, not until one of us breaks, and it will not be me.

# 22

Lucy

He pushes me away, and I am not sure why. Does he not want me anymore? No, that can't be true.

I sense the need in him, the want to tear into me, to break me. And I am not unhappy about it or threatened.

All I feel is a relief that finally he's revealed his true self to me. Just as I have to him. I watch him walk to the door, open it, and speak in a low voice to the soldier stationed outside. Footsteps approach up the corridor. A tray exchanges hands. He steps back, holding it. The door snicks shut behind him. It's a soft sound and yet it shivers over my sensitized skin. The scent of food wafts over to me, but that only twists my stomach.

He places the tray on the table, then turns and folds his arms over his chest. He doesn't say anything, just waits for me to comply with his unspoken command. Every line of his body indicates he'll patiently wait until I give in.

I want to say no, want to deny him, but all that comes out is a snarl. It's as if whatever I am becoming is cutting through the civilized veneer in me, marking me what I am. An omega with the desire to breed.

"You know what happens when you disobey me."

"So you'll fuck me?" I smirk. "Guess what, big man? That's what I want anyway."

"If you continue like this, I won't give you what you want."

What the —? My breath catches, and I feel the color leave my cheeks. "You wouldn't dare."

He bares his teeth, then grabs his crotch. "I can scent your arousal, the moisture that your body is producing as we speak."

His every word sends a fresh need rippling over my skin.

He growls, and the purr slashes through the hunger that has me in thrall. "Just my very nearness makes you want my cock thrusting inside you."

My spine arches back and my breasts grow heavy.

Every part of me wants to go to him, to throw myself at him and beg him to take me.

"And you will have it, but only when you do as you are told."

Rage thrums my nerve endings. That I needed him to fuck me and break my heat cycle is bad enough. That he taunts me about my dependency on him and holds back, is far worse. I feel like I am losing the very last of whatever pride I was holding on to. Pride? Hah! I have nothing left, nothing but this fiery will to fight back. To take what I need instead of always being put in a position where I am being manipulated and used.

Something inside me snaps.

I've had enough.

Enough.

I can't do this anymore. I can't always be the responsible one. The one who should provide for my sisters. The one who found a safe passage to this country. The one who negotiated with the leader of Scotland. The one who took the initiative to walk into this alpha's palace determined to see his demise. Not knowing it was my own that was in sight. If this is all that's left of me, then so be it. If I am reduced to this sniveling, wanting mass of emotions that cannot survive on my own anymore, then so be it.

I am tired of hiding what I am.

An omega who chooses to take.

A woman who will let herself feel.

A lover who will revel in her alpha's skin sliding over hers.

Who will be broken and filled again because she derives pleasure from it.

I am tired of asking. It's time I take what I need.

Everything around me fades. The room recedes. Everything except him. His scent, his face, those blue eyes that tear into my soul. It's all I can see. My gaze focuses in on him. Springing up on the bed, I run to the edge then jump across the space and throw myself at him.

His body sways. The breath slams out of him. He takes a step back but doesn't fall. He grabs my waist and holds me in place. I snap my legs around him, loop my arms over his shoulders, and fix my lips on his.

His mouth opens in surprise, and I slide my tongue in.

I drink of him, suck of his essence, I take from him and keep taking. I don't stop. At some point he responds. He yanks me close enough for my skin to rasp over his vest that he still hasn't removed. I smell blood in the air. Mine? His? I don't know.

A growl rumbles up his chest, flowing up our joined bodies. My thighs spasm and I dig my heels into the hard planes of his back.

He slants his head and sucks on my tongue.

The taste of him sinks into my mouth, flowing through my blood, and goes straight to my head.

Everything inside me comes alive.

My toes curl, and I dig my heels into his back. I am likely hurting myself, hurting him, too...and that doesn't matter. If anything, it only feeds that hunger inside me that is pushing to get out. That writhes and groans and wants more, so much.

I realize then I can't stop.

Not until I have him.

Not until I have it all. Not until I am in him, as he is in me. And it's not fair that this monster, this alpha who has the future of my clan in his hands is the one who can arouse these feelings of complete submission in me. But I am not submitting, am I?

All I am doing is tearing open my heart, my soul, my body, and offering it to him. And him? He takes.

Without tearing his mouth from mine, he walks to the bed. The world tilts; I feel the bed at my back. He pulls his mouth from mine and rises to his feet, putting distance between us.

My pulse quickens. Eyes half blind with desire, my senses alive with need, I move to rise with him. "No, please, don't..." Don't what? Don't go? Don't leave me? I want to say it out loud.

But that tiny, rational part of me that is still functioning holds me back. I have all but submitted my body to him, not my soul. Not my will. I cannot give him that. I will not put myself through the ultimate betrayal and give up everything. Not yet.

Tears prick the backs of my eyes, my chest feels like it is going to burst, and there is a growing pressure in my head. My brain cells seem to be melting, and surely, he can see it? Can't he tell how difficult this is for me? Can't he see how much I need this, need him? How much I want him to just take me, to give me the oblivion I so crave?

And maybe he does, because he cups my cheek. "Shh! I am not going anywhere. I just need to take off my clothes so I can feel you completely."

I swallow, registering the change in him. When did that happen? When did he go from being the aggressor to the comforter? I blink, and a teardrop runs down my cheek. His gaze follows it. Then he leans down and licks it up.

"You taste so sweet, so haunting." He brushes his lips over mine and straightens.

Every part of me wants to follow him, to fling myself back at him. But I wait. Wait.

I don't move. I can't take my gaze off him as he unhooks his vest.

Walking to the chair, he drapes it over the backrest.

The thick muscles of his triceps bulge. The scent of him deepens. Pungent, tangy, and so evocative. My mouth waters. The muscles low in my belly tighten. I clench my thighs but cannot stop the fresh burst of moisture that flows out. A low whine is drawn out of me.

I hear the keening need in it, and that turns me on further. "Hurry." My breath comes out in puffs. My chest rises and falls.

I want to lie back and shut my eyes, then fall into that black, yearning mass of need that is me. And yet a part of me cannot take my gaze away from the complete picture of maleness that is unfolding in front of me.

He slides the pants down and steps out of them.

Every part of me snaps to attention. My palms and feet tingle. I've seen him naked before, and yet the sheer poetry of those angles and planes of his body hits me anew. Heat flushes my skin. Every pore in my body is focused on him.

His wide back narrows to tight flanks that contract as he turns to face me.

I've sensed his strength, and yet the force of his dominance takes me by surprise.

He's so very male, every inch of him. My fingers twitch to grip his muscles and feel the unleashed power that hums under his skin.

His thighs are already taut with need, and between them his arousal which is large and veined. Saliva pools in my mouth. The size of him, the smell of his arousal, how he'd filled me earlier and pumped into me. The warmth of his cum filling my channel, his tongue thrusting into my mouth...the images flicker across my mind, speeding up. My breath comes in quick gasps. Sweat beads my palm. I know I am staring and I can't stop. Not even when he circles his shaft and runs his hand up the length. The slit glistens with beads of precum.

I lick my lips, wanting to taste him again.

I open my mouth to tell him, but all that emerges is a moan.

It seems to galvanize him into action, for he strides to the bed, leans above me, and rubs the liquid over my lips. "Tell me you want me."

I stare but can't stop myself from flicking out my tongue and slurping up the moisture.

His gaze grows lighter, and those irises of his turn almost colorless. "Say it. I'll give you what you need. All I need is to hear you say it now."

"No," I growl.

He holds my gaze.

And that connection is so hot, so unnerving that my hips seem to jerk forward of their own accord. I raise my pelvis, and scissor my legs around his waist so my core meets his cock. The swollen head of his shaft nudges the entrance of my wet channel, then he plunges inside.

## 23

Zeus

I plunge inside her.

Hot. Moist. Sensations spiral out from my groin. Warmth fills my chest. All my nerve endings seem to fire at once and I grit my teeth. The feeling is so different, so intimate. My muscles bunch, my throat closes, and...this can't be right.

It can't feel so good to be inside her, to have her pussy clamp around me and milk me. The need to pound into her is so strong, and yet, over-riding it is this need to protect. All emotions I have never experienced before, least of all for this omega whom I hadn't known until a few days ago.

My thigh muscles lock, and my biceps tremble as my arms support my body weight.

She digs her heels into my back. "What are you waiting for?" She bares her teeth.

And, really, she is only a tiny thing, less than half my size. And I am leaning over her, my muscles far stronger. It would take only one flick of my wrist to overpower her. The sheer audacity of her approach has me in thrall. I slide my fingers around her neck and grip it tightly.

If I wanted to, I could kill her right now.

Her gaze widens. The black pupils expand, not with fear...but arousal. A fresh pool of slick spurts out of her and coils around my cock. I grow bigger and fill her up inside, until my hardening flesh brushes against the walls of her womb. She groans. So do I.

She flings back her head, her neck arches, and she bites down on her lips. And that sends me over the edge. I pull out of her and stay poised at the entrance to her wet channel.

I know I am going to hurt her and yet I can't stop myself. Her gaze widens. She mewls, scrunching up her face, and her cheeks flush...with anger? With desire. She peels back her lips and digs her fingernails into the back of my shoulder.

"Don't you stop now, Alpha. Or else—"

"Or else?" I growl and more moisture gushes from her.

Her eyes roll back, and she moans. "Or else, I'll never spread my legs for you again, not willingly."

I almost laugh aloud. Oh, the irony! She is throwing my words back at me.

Her chest heaves, and her breasts rise and fall, the nipples hard enough to scratch a furrow down my skin.

Does she really believe that she has a choice in how she'll submit to me? That she could hint at that should bother me, but it doesn't. Not as much as the sheer possessiveness that grips me. I lean in close and pinch her chin, forcing her head down. She cracks her eyes open, the green a ring around the darkness of her pupils almost filling her entire eyes.

"Whenever I want, however I want, I'll fuck you, and you'll take it all."

She pauses; her breath hitches.

I lower my voice. "And you'll ask for more."

Her eyes dilate until the green completely vanishes. The color fades from her cheeks. The honeyed scent of her arousal deepens, laced with the acrid scent of fear. And I want to soothe her and tell her I'll never hurt her.

Even as a part of me is pleased that she is still afraid of me. She should be, for she has no idea how close I am to binding her to me and never letting her go.

It would serve her right if I did.

I should.

Bind her. Knot her to me. So she can never belong to anyone else. "No one but me," I snarl. My voice slices through the haze in my head. "Do you understand?"

She nods.

"Tell me." Why is it so important that I hear her acknowledge my dominance? I am not sure. Except that possessive part of me, the one that demands her complete subjugation, wants her to say it aloud. Craves it with a fierceness I can't fathom. But I can't fight it either—I don't want to fight it.

"Yes" she snaps, tears glittering in her eyes.

"Yes, what?"

"Yes, Alpha." She hisses through lips bitten from my ministrations.

A part of me registers the anger and the frustration that emanates from her. But I ignore it all.

"My name. Say my name."

She grits her teeth and sets her chin. Her eyes glow with that light of stubbornness that both frustrates and also excites me.

"Say it." I harden my jaw, knowing I am dangerously gone in my passion, in my anger; knowing that I am on the verge of hurting her in the middle of my lust, and yet I know there is no turning back. Not now.

She clenches the walls of her pussy around my dick.

A fierce surge of desire tugs my groin. Lust flows down my spine, filling my balls until I am hurting. Until I know I can't hold back.

I growl loudly and her stomach muscles cramp. Her body responds to my every nuance. I know I am taking advantage of the fact that I have pinned her in place. That I can control her body as easily as I can control my own. Too bad I can't tame her mind or her spirit. Yet a part of me rejoices at the challenge. Knowing there can be no other mate for me.

Mate?

Yes, she is, and no, it doesn't mean anything.

It's the most convenient way of keeping her with me.

My lips twist in derision at myself. At the sorry man I have become. One reduced to trying to subdue the one thing that has come into my life and has sparked the urge to fight again, for myself, for her. For everything I hold dear. I feel more alive than I ever have before.

As alive as the day I killed my father and took revenge for my mother's death.

"Say. It." I growl once more and deepen my purr.

This time I feel the slick gather at the base of her core. Feel the hunger that rips through her so her back arches and her breasts thrust up. Her nipples tighten. Her hips tremble. The scent of her arousal flows over me. Crashes over me, tightening my need. Stretching it until I am sure I am going to snap. I can't hold back. I can't. And yet... "Please." The word dribbles out; my voice breaks.

"Zeus," she whispers on a breath.

The sound of my name from her lips sends a pulse of desire tearing down my spine. The blood thunders at my temples, my shoulders bunch, and every muscle in my body tenses in preparation. I will invade her, take her, fucking own her. I must. Liquid lust rams through my blood demanding that she scream when I do so. Knowing she will throw her head back, kick her heels into my back, dig her nails into my neck, and tear grooves down my skin when I rut her, and all of it sends me over the edge.

I plunge into her, sinking all the way inside her melting channel. I tilt my hips, and grind myself in to the hilt. The blood rushes to my groin. The bulbous knot at the base of my shaft swells. I thrust forward that last millimeter and hook behind her pelvic bone, locking her to me. Her body bucks and her pussy clamps onto my turgid flesh, drawing me in even closer. Tight. Hot. Succulent. Mine. The feel of it, the complete rightness of it floods me, filling every last cell in my body and overflowing. My balls draw up, my thigh muscles spasm and I want to come inside her, mark her, claim her and yet something makes me wait. Wait. Leaning down, I take her lips, thrust my tongue inside her sweet mouth, and rake my fingers through her hair.

Her little body goes stiff, and then I feel her climax shudder up from her toes, sweeping over her thighs, pinning her waist to the bed, her chest vibrating, then her throat ripples, and she screams, and I absorb it all. Only then do I let the hot streams of cum gush forth as I empty myself inside her.

## 24

Lucy

When I come to it is to the thud of his heart under my cheek. I slide my fingers over warm skin. Turn my face and bury my nose in the light smattering of hair on his chest.

The scent of his sweat and musk of his arousal turns me on, and it also strangely soothes me. I feel protected and cherished, and the still thinking part of my mind warns me I am falling into a place from which there is no return. I try to move only to find there is a heavy weight around my waist. It's his arm, which is massive enough to hold me down.

It feels so right that I know it's wrong.

Not like this.

All my life I've spent fighting that core inside me, the part that was intrinsically omega that needed to be tamed, subdued, knotted, and bred. And in one stroke he…this alpha, the most monstrous of all in the city, has done just that. And I had encouraged him. The faint recollection of giving him what he wanted, of calling him by his name tumbles over me.

My cheeks flush.

That is more intimate than anything else we've done.

And it shouldn't be.

I'd called him by his name, that's all. We all have one. Then why does it feel like I have broken a pact with myself? That I have gone back on the promise made to my clan, that I have betrayed myself by doing that?

I wriggle against the massive chest of the alpha, and he doesn't let go. Big surprise.

He folds his other arm around me and purrs. The sound is low, and soft, and flows over my skin. Its soothing in a way it shouldn't be. He rubs my back as if trying to pacify me. He rests his chin on my head, and I have this insane need to bury myself in his chest, to surround myself with his warmth and his heat, to draw that shroud of protectiveness over me and let it consume me. I squeeze my eyes shut, not sure why I feel the need to cry. It's only my life that will never be the same. A sob catches in my throat. My shoulders shudder as I try to bite my lips, try to consume every last depressing emotion that wells up. What is happening to me?

The giant purrs once more, and the sound instantly sinks into my blood.

The tension drips out of me, and my shoulders sag. No, no. I don't want that to happen.

I don't want him to be able to manipulate me such that even my grief is something that is not my own.

I want to rage at him and tell him that.

Instead, I let the tears flow down my cheeks. The warmth pools on his chest, and he must feel it, for he firms his hold on me.

"You are upset at how you responded to me." His breath raises the hair on my head. "Don't be."

He runs his palm from the nape of my neck down to my hips and back up again. The moment is soothing, and soft...tender. "You are the most passionate woman I have ever met."

He praises me.

And it's all wrong. He's not meant to soothe me or take care of me. He's meant to overwhelm and threaten and force himself on me. Truth is, he didn't do anything I didn't want. Even now, caught up in the throes of the end of my heat cycle, with my mind half hazy with the need for him, with my body already signaling that I need the alpha to fuck me again, the rational part of my brain insists that I can't put all the blame on him.

Perhaps I had been stupid to walk into his lair and let myself be caught by him, and yes, he had taken me, but everything that had happened after that, I had wanted it.

I can't blame myself for getting caught, for as soon as I had seen him, had sniffed his luscious alpha scent, I'd known it was him. Only I had been denying it to myself so far.

The thought quiets me...my muscles relax, my toes uncurl. I let my body sag against him.

Zeus seems satisfied by the response, but he doesn't stop his purring. His large palm continues to soothe me. He drags his fingers through my hair, scraping his fingernails across my scalp. Ripples of pleasure undulate down my spine. A moan dribbles out of me.

I sense the change in him at that. Feel the hardness that nudges against my hip.

He rakes his fingers over my nape, over my spine, cupping the curve of my hips before sliding his hand into the space between my legs. I can't stop the groan that wells up. My thigh muscles clench, locking his fingers in place.

Moisture pools inside my core and trickles down my thigh. I know this time it's not his purring or his cajoling that has drawn out the slickness from me. It's me enjoying his body, his nearness, his presence. It's the way he's tried to claim me, tried to draw the uncertainty from me.

And I feel grateful. There. I've acknowledged it to myself. I am grateful that he found me in the middle of my heat cycle, that I had gone into my heat cycle right there in his presence, that he had taken me and helped me through it, that it is him who broke me and knotted me. My sisters... The thought of them waiting crashes through my head, and I push it away. I need to get to them, and I will get to them. But I need to use this to my advantage. Clearly, he wants me, he finds me attractive, he claimed me, and the only thing I can do is use this to help my clan. Barter my submission for them. Pretend an acquiescence I don't really feel, to draw him into his comfort zone, until he lets his guard down, and then... My muscles tense.

A growl rumbles up from him. His hands grip my waist and, lifting me up, he slides me down the thick girth of his shaft.

Just like that, he fills me, the hard, engorged flesh dragging against my softer inner walls, sending a pulse of desire up my spine. Little bursts of flame explode behind my eyes. I moan at the feeling of being completely full, and the sound of his growl twines with mine.

He raises and lowers me on his shaft, and again. Desire thrums my nerves, liquid heat pools in my core, and I clench my inner walls around him. I can't stop, not even if I wanted to. I am rewarded with another snarl from the alpha.

"Look at me."

I open my eyes and am caught in the swirling depths of his silver gaze. Flickers of gold spark in their depths. It captures me, holds me in thrall. When he slides his hand up to grip my nape and brings my face forward, I don't resist.

Not even when he holds me there, poised over him, staring down into his face, my position that of mock dominance, but I am not fooled. He controls me, his anger holds me in check, the feeling of unleashed power that hums under his skin binds me to him, and the low hum of the mating cord under my rib cage tells me I am his as much as he is mine.

He lowers me down his shaft until my hips slide over his. I grip the sides of his waist with my knees and squeeze my inner walls. The burst of gold in his eyes glows brighter, and it feels...so good that I can give him pleasure. I squeeze again. A groan rumbles up his massive chest, color burning high on his cheeks.

Just like that, the sexual tension ratchets up. His nostrils flare, his eyes narrow and his gaze falls to my breasts. He flips me over so I am under him and without pulling out of me,he leans down and bites my nipple. Flares of need sizzle over my skin, leaving little sparks of fire in their wake. My eyelids flutter down.

"No."

The command in his voice whips through my mind, and my eyelids snap open. My gaze is caught in his.

"Mine," he growls.

I swallow. Something stretched tight inside me dissolves.

He hooks his hands under my knees, yanking my legs up and over his shoulders, so I am spread wide. I thrust my hips up, and the angle means he slides in deep. Deeper than he's ever been before. It feels like he is piercing me in half. He seems to touch the very secret core in me where no one has, where no one else will ever be, no one but him. Why does it feel like he's ripped off every single mask I've worn to the world and made me his?

Something seems to change in him, too, for he lowers his head and slants his lips over mine. He thrusts his tongue into my mouth, and his cock expands inside.

The knot snaps into place.

Like it was meant to happen. I know then that everything that has happened in my life has brought me up to this point: to submit to him, to give him pleasure, even as I take from him.

My soft core tightens around him, milking him, and the climax slithers out from my center, flooding me, embracing me as the thick juice of his cum bathes my channel. His big body shudders; the muscles of his back clench.

He kisses the edge of my mouth, the gesture almost tender, then he rests his forehead on mine. A bead of sweat drizzles down his temple. I flick my tongue out to lick it up.

"Yours."

I only realize that I've said the word aloud when he stills over me. Then he scoops me up and turns me over to rest on his chest. He runs his palm over my hair. Once again, his touch feels almost tender. But that's not possible. Surely, I am mistaken. The most brutal alpha in this part of the world is not capable of a soft touch. He is not.

Is he?

"Sleep now and recover your strength." His voice sinks into my blood.

There is a subtle command to the words that insists I obey him. I want to resist him, and yet, this once…just once, will it not be okay to shut my eyes and give in to this feeling of warmth and comfort and safety which cocoons me? Can I not give in to that part of me that wants to be owned?

When I wake up, I am alone.

# 25

Zeus

I walk into the war room for the daily recon to find the place is empty, except for Ethan. He rises to his feet as I walk in. I slow my steps.

It's not in the man to be that formal. Oh, he respects me all right, only he's not given to such outward gestures, not when we are on our own.

I pull out a chair, drop into it, and tip it all the way back. "Kayden is preparing to attack?"

Ethan goes still; his gaze narrows.

"Don't be so surprised, Second." I set the chair on its front legs with a thump. "The fucker is bound to spring that on us when we least expect it—"

"Namely right after initiating the peace talks?" Ethan frowns. "Why am I not surprised that you'd have already anticipated it?"

"Admit it, you are impressed." I push back the chair, then prop my legs on the table.

Ethan watches me with a frown. "That's an antique table."

Boo fucking hoo. I scratch my chin. Nevertheless, I swing my legs off the table and set my feet on the floor with a snap. "You're delaying the inevitable, Second."

"Oh, what the fuck." Ethan shifts his weight from one foot to the other. "Fine, I am impressed."

I drum my fingers on the table. "Why do I feel a 'but' coming on?"

"You are so able to anticipate Kayden's moves. Sometimes I think the two of you have some kind of a past that I don't know anything about."

My shoulders freeze. "How did you guess?"

"What the fuck?" Ethan's features harden. He marches to the table and pounds his fist on the surface. "Why didn't you tell me anything about this until now? Do you know how important this piece of information is to the future of this city, for the future of coming generations? For—"

"Relax, brother," I drawl. "I was yanking your chain."

"Oh, for fuck's sake!" Color rushes to his cheeks

"Calm down, asshole. At this rate, you'll have a coronary and die in this room instead of going out with a bang in a fight."

"Is that what you want, to meet a bloody end?" He leans down and grabs my collar. "Is this why you can't wait to leap into a fight with Kayden, so the two of you can slaughter each other?"

"You want a fight, Second? You only have to ask." I hold his gaze. And it feels weird that I am calm while Ethan, the sensible one, is all worked up. "If I didn't know better, I'd think you were worried about losing me."

"Oh, bloody fuck." He lets go of me and steps back.

"Can't remember when you used that four-letter word so many times in one conversation last." I grin.

"What-fucking-ever." He rakes his fingers through his hair, but his eyebrows draw down.

"Now you are borrowing my dialogue." I click my tongue. "Really, E, it's time you think of something more original."

"Time you think of how we put an end to this Kayden-shaped problem. It's bad enough that you took the omega to bed—"

"What's your point?" I crack my neck from side to side. My shoulders flex. Ethan's right, much as I hate to admit it. Kayden had sent the omega to kill me...and I had mated her.

What a fucking mess. "The bastard is as much in my head as I am in his," I growl, more disturbed than I want to let on.

Our two countries have been at war for so long that I'd known it would come to this—a bloody battle which I intend to win. Not for my Council or the citizens of this fair city. I don't owe any of them anything. Nope, it's my pride that insists I defeat Kayden, quash any resistance. That and being able to use his resources to restructure this city. Wipe it clean of the dirt and muck, the corruption that grabs at its roots. I am so close now, to getting what I want, I can taste it. The fine hairs on my neck harden. I drum my fingers over my chest. It can't be that simple.

Kayden couldn't have been so careless that news of his plans would so conveniently reach me, giving me time to plan a defense.

I rise to my feet, only to pace along the length of the room.

Ethan watches, his gaze hard. "Aren't you going to gloat we should have listened to you and attacked a few days ago when you first mentioned that offense was the best form of defense?"

I pause and swivel around on my heels. "It's not in me to strike a man when he is down...not." I peel my lips back at him, let the glint of satisfaction show in my eyes.

"It's clear we need to get our troops together, to prepare for a fight." He turns to leave.

"No."

He pauses mid-step, then shoots me a glance. "*Excuse me?*"

So fucking polite. I much prefer the Ethan who says what is on his mind. But then he's the gentleman, trained in the etiquette that makes him the kind of alpha that omegas yearn for.

Me? I am the marauder, the one who takes. Who protects, too—not that I'd ever admit to that—just without the finer points of behavior that Ethan can lay claim to.

"You heard me." I rub the back of my neck. "How many people know of this?"

"Just you and me, and the spy who brought the news."

"Keep it that way." I set my jaw.

"What are you playing at, Zeus?" He frowns.

"You knew what you were getting when you chose me. You know I don't trust anyone with my plans."

"A strength."

I nod.

"Except when it isn't. When you hold your cards too close to your chest, when you don't allow anyone else to see what you are, then what you become is a dictator."

"Right on first count." I chuckle, the sound harsh. "I have never tried to hide what I am. I am not the idealized version of the leader you think I am.

"You are not a monster, Zeus." He leans forward on his feet, his gaze measured, his chin rock-hard.

"I didn't take you for an ass-licker either." I grin.

"You are too smart," he continues as if I hadn't spoken, "too intelligent to waste your position, the title you carry, your bloodline…you wouldn't use it without reason. You have a plan all right. It's just not the one you are sharing with me and the Council. And unlike them—"

"You're not gullible." A smile tugs my lips, the first genuine one of the day since I fondled the omega and touched her face and reluctantly left her sleeping in the bed stained from the evidence of our rutting.

I shouldn't let thoughts of her interrupt this important session. This is the reason I've fought so far, the reason I'd overthrown the old order, brought in people of my own, cultivated the city. And yet when the goal is so close, when I can all but taste the revenge, the fruit of my years of struggling, all I can think about is her.

"You are losing your focus." He grimaces. "*She* is making you lose your concentration." And the smile on his face is one of satisfaction. As if he's been waiting so long to see me fall. He'll relish every last second of seeing me drown in the feelings that are engulfing me.

"I hear every word you say, friend." I emphasize the last word, making it a mockery of what it is meant to be. "Do not for a second think I have lost sight of what I want."

"Except what you wanted forty-eight hours ago…is it the same as what you want now?"

"Of course it is. I—" The words cease. Something very much like an epiphany sweeps over me. He's right. It's not sufficient to kill Kayden. Not adequate to raze this city to the ground. Not enough to organize for those who are loyal to me to be part of the new world I hope to build. No, there is something more. Her. I need her with me. Want her close by so I can bury myself in her sweet cunt when the need takes me. So I can feel her soft skin, twine the silky hair around my fingers, see her grow fat with my child, and kiss her and love her and mate her and… Sweat beads my brow. My vest sticks to my back. The heat in the room is suddenly too much to bear.

I stalk to the window and fling it open, leaning outside. I'd never done this before, looking for fresh air in a city where there is none. Where the smoke from the charcoal fires that people burn at night to keep warm settles over the space, coating everyone in fine grime.

Where a deep breath in the open will clog the pores on your skin. Yet I find myself leaning out and gasping lungfuls of the pollution. Laced below the pea-soup fog I smell the moisture from the Thames. The sluggish brown sludge of the river flows in the distance. Over the years the water has reduced to a trickle of what it was. The ruins of the bridge that had been destroyed by the bombs mock me from a distance.

There's a touch on my shoulder, and I know it's Ethan.

"A mating bond goes both ways, or didn't you realize that."

He's right, and yet a part of me doesn't want to accept it. The mating bond was not spontaneous. It was something I had decided on the moment I'd set eyes on her. I'd known that I was going to claim her. And yet I shake his hand off.

"You gloating now?" I turn on him.

"You know I don't do that." He puts up his palms.

"Yeah, you leave the finer points of being an asshole to me."

"Like I said, you are a better man than you give yourself credit for." He grips my shoulder, his gaze serious.

I almost tell him what I have in mind for the city then. Almost. "You're wrong." I step back. "You don't have to worry that this will derail our plan to fight the Scots."

"I never doubted that anything would take your mind off the goal at the end." His voice is sincere. He sounds exactly like the Ethan I know.

"Power. Ultimate power, that's all I crave." I say it aloud and I know it's to remind myself of what I have at stake.

A way to help focus my mind which insists on reaching out through the mating bond to her.

As if sensing my interest, the mating bond twangs. Grief and loneliness sweep through. It twists my heart. A band of ice tightens around my chest.

A feeling of such utter dejectedness crawls into my gut, and I know without a doubt it is her. That the omega is awake and needs comforting and tending. Likely she is coming down after the high of the heat cycle. As the reality of what has been done sinks into her, she will rebel and try to escape. And I cannot, will not let that happen. "I need to go to her."

My gaze snaps on Ethan. My voice sounds hollow and desperate, and I don't try to mask it.

"It's normal for the first months of a newly paired bond for each to be so attuned to the other that you have difficulty telling your emotions apart from hers."

His voice is solicitous, and it should soothe me that he is trying to calm me. Instead, a burst of anger twists my insides. "And how would you know that?" I snap.

His gaze widens, but there is no other change in expression. "So I have heard. Consider it advice from one friend to another. The crux of my experience should help an alpha who is about to enter a very tumultuous stage of a relationship, one that will affect your mind and hence the plans that the entire Council has worked on so meticulously over months."

I look at his features, trying to detect any trace of the fact that he was making fun of me, or that he was speaking in jest, but all I see is seriousness, a trace of concern perhaps. I drop my hands and step back. "Advice accepted."

I swerve around him and head for the door.

"I let go of the omega who could have been my mate and I will forever regret it."

I pause at the exit, then turn to him. "She's—"

"Alive. I met her on my last trip to Russia, was attracted to her instantly, wanted to claim her…" His voice trails off.

"But you didn't." I angle my head, watching him closely.

His lips firm. A pulse ticks above his jaw. "I waited too long. I didn't act on my instinct. When I went back in search of her she was gone. The Vikings invaded Russia and all hell broke loose. They caught me and almost killed me. Only let me go when they realized I was your second." His lips twist. "Even those barbarians did not want to cause a diplomatic incident with you."

"My reputation precedes me." I should feel a fierce surge of pride that news of how I had taken power in London had traveled that far. I should feel gratified that the fiercest warriors in the land hesitate to challenge me. Instead, all I can think of is the softness of her curves under my fingers. Smell the scent of her arousal as I bury my nose in her core, the taste of her essence as I lick her moist folds. And all of it insists that there is more to life than absolute power.

How can I think that? I roll my shoulders and try to school my thoughts into some semblance of familiarity. Soon I'll be taking pity on my own people, pardoning their faults, rebuilding the infrastructure for them, and what the fuck? Obviously, the proximity to the omega is softening me up.

"So you see, I understand a little of what you are going through… Hell, I am envious that you found an omega who calls to you the way she does." He drags his fingers through his hair. "And ignore what I said earlier. Ultimately if she is the woman for you, then nothing else matters, certainly not the fact that Kayden sent her to kill you."

"And the surprises keep coming." So not what I'd expected to hear from Ethan. That must have cost him, given how much he hates the Scots. This fight with Kayden is personal for him. For me…it's a means to show the world I am better than my father.

"We'll find her." I stalk back to him. "I'll help you find her." I grip his shoulder.

His gaze widens. Guess he hadn't expected me to say that. Hell, I hadn't expected myself to say that. The omega's influence is more consuming than I realized.

The mating bond stutters, and a cold feeling coils in my gut. My shoulders stiffen, and I half turn toward the exit.

Ethan's eyebrows furrow. "Go." He jerks his chin to the door.

I don't question the urgency that sweeps through my blood. She needs me. Swiveling around, I rush for the exit.

# 26

Lucy

I look at myself in the mirror and wince. My hair is caked with cum, and there is fluid drying on my body. My lips are swollen, the skin around my lips is chafed, my nipples look unusually larger, and my breasts...?

I cup them and grimace.

They feel sore, like they have been squeezed and pummeled.

Well, to be fair, he had been gentle with my breasts. Overall, he'd been gentle with my body. For a big man like him, his fingers are unusually light in their touch. He'd rubbed his cum into every part of me that he could access, then poured some of our joined-up liquids into my mouth, and I had...loved it.

I admit it.

I had relished every touch, feel, taste of him.

I had reveled in his scent. I had fucked him right back.

I grasp the edge of the wash basin and lean forward, my hair falling over my face, bringing with it the scent of sex. That darker, deeper, muskier essence of his laced with the lighter one that I recognize as the spoor of my own arousal.

It feels like he's right here with me in the room again. His scent, his touch, his caresses surround me. My lower belly cramps, and liquid seeps out from between my legs.

I squeeze my eyes shut and will back the sickness that twists my gut. The mating bond twangs and coils inside, trying to reassure me that this is as it should be, that he is my mate, he had taken me, used me. Claimed me. It is only right that my body responds to him.

No, no, no. I swing out and smash my fist into the mirror. Cracks spider over the surface and pain slices through the sexual haze that has gripped me. Scarlet drips down my fingers and splashes on the floor dripping over the shards of broken glass. I swear bring the side of my palm to my mouth and suck on it. I have made a mess of this place. Is he going to punish me for this? Probably. Most likely he'll fuck me again, and my body will enjoy it and ask for more.

My shoulders hunch, and the adrenaline fades. I am bleeding, and I know I need to stop the flow of blood, and yet my legs feel too heavy to move.

Every part of my body aches.

Not surprising, though, for it's been what, five, six days since he brought me here and locked me in his space? Since he ravished me and forced the mating bond on me?

I only have myself to blame. I made the first move. I bit him, I staked my need for the bond. It was the heat cycle, of course, and I can keep telling myself that.

That my hormones are at play and I am not really aware of what is happening. It doesn't change the reality of everything that has taken place.

Tears burn at the backs of my eyes and fall on my hand, burning the broken skin that still bleeds. I need to get ahold of myself. The bond twinges again, and a feeling of warmth pours down it, bleeding into my muscles. It's as if he knows of my discomfort and is trying to soothe me. Lies, all lies. I don't trust him. All of it: his taking care of me, making sure I am fed, trying to get me to say his name, seducing me by sharing a little bit of the broken man I sense inside the monster on the outside. All of it is an act.

I feel his presence creeping under my skin, twinning with my blood. He's becoming a part of me.

Just as he'd rubbed his fluids into every crevice on my body, making sure to strengthen the bonding process. Making me a part of him, too. The thought sends a shudder of fear down my spine. I am losing myself in the omega I am at heart. That core of me who is bonded to an alpha, who wants to be taken and cared for. Who needs an alpha to rut her through a cycle. I am all of that and more. So much more. I need to stop resisting him. Need to let him in, let him take, allow myself to dissolve into him... then find myself again.

I stare at the woman whose face is reflected in the cracked mirror. Something inside me tells me I am right. The sooner I put this plan in action, the faster I can find a grip on my destiny, find a way to help my sisters. All without telling him. If I tell him the real reason I am here, he'll only find a way to get to my clan, many of whom are omegas like me. He'd make them join his harem, and I am not that stupid.

No, I need to play him at his own game.

He wants an omega? A meek woman? A breeder? I'll become that. I'll throw him off my track, then find a way to get what I want. I must bide my time until I find a weakness and then I am going to kill him...break the bond he forced on me.

The mating cord writhes at the thought, sending a shudder of pain so sharp that I double over. My body cannot stand the thought of him dying. Every second I am here with him, in his room, every time he fucks me, cares for me, makes me think of him, the bond only deepens. I need to kill him before the bond becomes so strong that his dying would kill me, too. I have no intention of dying, not like this.

Turning, I walk to the shower closet, wrench the door open, and step in. The water is blissfully hot, and I let it pour over me, let it clean away the residue of the various times he took me.

My skin is so sensitive that the water sliding over it sends a shiver of need coursing through me.

The wound at the base of my neck where he bit me throbs. I had avoided looking at the broken skin in the mirror. Trying to deny what he'd done to me. I needn't have bothered.

The wound softens under the water and pulses with need. It seems to be calling for its maker to touch it, caress it, and soothe away the pain. The cord in my chest pulses, and a dense plume of heat flushes my skin. I imagine I hear his purring, feel his massive chest at my back, his arm a steel band around my waist, sliding up until his big palm cups my breast, tweaking my nipple.

His other palm slides down to part my lower lips. He drags his fingers through the folds, slipping into my wet, needy channel. Heat coils low, tightening my belly, and I lean forward to rest my forehead against the wall.

His presence only follows me. His big body shields me from the shower. His lips touch the claiming marks—he licks it, his saliva sealing the wound. The pain recedes and is replaced by pure primal greed. For him. To take me all over again. It shouldn't be possible to want him again. Not after the number of times, he's taken me already.

Not after I'd allowed myself to be used over and over again. And not after my heat cycle has simmered to an end, and yet here I am, in the shower imagining he is here with me and…

"You can't shut me out." His breath shudders over the shell of my ear.

The hair on my nape rises. It was him all along. He'd been here with me, and I'd known it and yet I'd tried to ignore it. Hoping if I pretended enough, he wouldn't actually be here…if I tried enough, I'd forget everything that had happened to me.

I sense his presence pull at me through the bond, feel his need seep through my blood, my soul, and I know then, as much as I pretend, things will never be the same. That I can't hide from him, or from myself. He places his palm over my hand, then spreads my fingers flush against the shower wall before doing the same with the other.

Trailing his hands over my arms, he traces the lines toward my back, down my spine to the curve of my hips.

I sense him sink to his knees, then he licks the swell of my butt to where the cheeks part in the middle.

Desire thuds at my nerves. I feel the blood rush to my face and huh, why am I blushing now? He's already done so much to my body, he knows every inch of my skin, and yet as he parts my butt cheeks and slips his tongue into the puckered hole there, I find my muscles clenching. I press my fingers into the stone wall. His arm wraps around my front, and he skims his fingers through my core, his touch gentle, almost comforting. He thrusts a thumb into my soaking channel, and I moan, my lower belly stuttering then unfurling. He moves his other arm up to cup my breast, caress it, tweak it.

The first stirrings of a climax tremble up from my soles.

I shudder, and my knees quake. He seems to sense it, too, for he grips my hips and turns me around.

Before I can crack my eyes open, he spreads my thighs apart, then flips one of my legs over his shoulder.

Then he plunges his tongue into my wet core, sucking, nibbling, biting on my clit.

The climax surges up my spine and sweeps over my nape to break into little flickers of light behind my closed eyelids.

My other knee gives out from under me, and I slide down against the shower wall, only for him to rise, and prop me up. He wraps my legs around his waist, angles his hips and plunges into me, again and again.

I can't stop myself from holding on to his broad shoulders, from burying my teeth into his shoulder, from groaning, moaning his name, and letting the slickness flow out to welcome him as his knot locks into place.

His groan echoes over the sound of the shower and he pours his very essence into me.

We stay that way, joined up until the water runs cold.

Then he flicks off the shower and, with him still inside me, steps out of the stall. He grabs a towel and covers me with it, running it over my back, my hair.

I cling to him, refusing to open my eyes, letting the tiredness tug me under, allowing him to care for me again. Knowing I must protest. Knowing I will take every last drop of concern he shows me, and hating myself anyway.

This time when sleep claims me, I embrace it just as I embrace the monster to whose chest I cling as I burrow into it.

When I wake, I am alone in bed.

I watch him as he works out in a corner of the room, naked from the waist up. Seeing the light that filters through the window to frame him, lighting the honey brown of his skin, tracing the scars that mark his back, the tattoos on his arms that move with each ripple of his muscle, I realize he is not only powerful but there is a certain poetry to how he moves. A fluidity. He goes through what is clearly a morning routine…a mix of tai chi and calisthenics and yoga, which seem easy to follow but I know must take complete concentration.

Sweat glistening on his shoulders, he finally stretches out. There's a knock at the door, and the alpha I'd noticed when I'd broken into the Ascension ceremony walks in.

Zeus crosses the room and takes the tray of food from him. He shoves his considerable bulk in front of the other alpha, shutting out the room and me from sight.

They speak low enough that I cannot decipher the words. The man nods, then leaves without a glance in my direction.

When Zeus turns, his gaze locks with mine.

I expect him to command me to eat… To drink… To fuck… To sleep?

I brace myself for his touch, for him to show me again that he is more powerful, my alpha. Instead, he swaggers to the table by the window and slides the tray onto it. He slugs down half a bottle of water, then places it back on the table. He grabs up the vest that's flung over the chair and shrugs it on, then drops into the chair. Reaching for the pot of coffee, he pours himself a cup.

A tangy, bitter aroma fills the space. My nostrils twitch, and my mouth waters.

He takes a sip of the steaming liquid and his eyes close in appreciation. My stomach growls. The bastard's not going to offer it to me. I need to go there and get it for myself. I swing my feet over, looking around for clothes. There are none, except for a shirt that belongs to him. Standing, I reach for it, pull it on. It dwarfs me, and the fabric smells like him. It feels like I am wrapped up in layers of his essence. I open my mouth to protest then pause. I need him to think that I am accepting my situation. Crossing over, I slide into the chair opposite him.

"Good morning." I pour myself a cup of coffee. So fucking civil. I sound so fake even to my own ears, he's going to see right through me.

He nods at me over his cup.

Well, what do you know? He's buying my act?

His lips curve up, and the skin around his eye's crinkles. He's been expecting me to fall in with his plans all along.

I curl my fingers around the cup and very much want to fling it at him. Instead, I lower it and place it carefully on the table.

Reaching for a buttery croissant, I drop one on his plate, then slide another onto mine and break it.

"I don't trust this supplication from you." He leans back in his chair. "What is it you really want, Lucia Erasmus, Czarina of Russia. Why are you really here?"

# 27

Lucy

I pause with the croissant halfway to my lips, and stare at him.

Spit drools from my open mouth.

For once, all of the graces instilled in me since childhood, since I was brought up as the treasured omega in the household of the Czar of Russia, desert me. But then it has been a long time since anyone has called me by my full name. The name which I'd hoped I'd left behind when I escaped from Russia.

I'd run away from the arrangement my father had in mind for me… straight into a bond with an alpha who is much more fearsome.

Why is it that everywhere I turn there is always a man who wants to hold me down, collar me, bond to me, make me feel like I am secondary, only an omega?

*'You're not an average omega…'* My mother's voice echoes in my ears. *'You are a pure-born omega who carries in your blood the genes of the Russian royal family. The genes that guarantee your offspring will not only be strong but be resis-*

*tant to most diseases, blessed with the ability to foresee, a kind of intuition that many would kill for.'*

And yet I hadn't foreseen my own future, that I would walk straight into this trap, have an alpha cage me, bond to me.

Or was that why I had brokered the deal with Kayden, knowing I couldn't possibly trust the Scottish alpha? Knowing it would be a trap, that he was bound to claim me? No, even before. From the time I first heard my father mention Zeus' name, talk about his prowess and how he'd taken over as General, I'd known an affinity for him right from then.

I had refused to accept it. Not until I'd walked into that grand hall and seen him and scented him and then…then there had been no turning back. I'd known then I was his.

"You…" The piece of croissant slips from my fingers and falls to the plate. "How long have you known?" I pick up the piece and pop it back into my mouth. I can't taste it, yet I force myself to bite into it, chew it, then swallow.

Zeus tilts his head and surveys me with that steady gaze.

"Your second, he told you…" I don't need to look at him to sense him nod his confirmation.

I reach for the coffee cup and drain it. And, damn it, I should be raging, or be afraid or throw a tantrum, or something. Yet all I feel is a strange calm.

I'd known it would come to this, had known inside, that from the time I'd walked into his stronghold, this confrontation was coming. Or perhaps it I'd lost every shred of feeling, of my identity, when I had gone into heat, had crawled into that bed with him and asked him to take me.

When my body had led the way forward and the rest of me had no choice but to follow.

When everything I'd learned about myself, my self-respect, my pride… all of it had been swept aside in that carnal need to mate. Because ultimately that's what I am deep inside, a female whose omega instinct will always be in the lead.

"Don't you have anything else to say for it?" His voice is low, his gaze steady. He hasn't eaten anything on his plate so far either.

And I don't know why that simple detail sticks in my head. Either he's more upset than he's letting on… Or, nope, can't be that. He had a need, he sensed me, he wanted me, he took me. There's nothing more to it than that. He can't possibly be upset about the fact that my identity was a surprise to him.

"You don't seem surprised?" I want to be as casual as him and reach for the rest of the croissant, but my stomach suddenly feels heavy, my guts lurching. I lean back and rub my forearms.

"Should I be?" He places his elbows on the table.

"Shouldn't you?" I raise my eyes and meet his gaze.

His cheekbones stand out in relief. Some of the color has faded from his face. It only makes his features look more austere, more brooding. He seems strong and powerful and formidable. Waves of tension roll off him. I sense a pulse of heat and something else… A spark of anger rolls down the mating bond; it tugs at my nerve endings. I wriggle around in my chair, trying to find a more comfortable position. I shouldn't feel so guilty, I shouldn't. I am not the one at fault. I am only trying to do right by my clan, aren't I? Then why does his very presence make me feel like I tried to pull a fast one on him? That I lied to him?

"I did not…" Only when I hear the words aloud do I realize I have spoken.

He angles his head. His eyes darken into flints of ice. So cold. So terrifying.

He can be far more formidable than he's alluded to.

He'd taken me against my will and yet he'd also cared for me. He'd made sure to rut me through the cycle, had never hit me or abused me. Why am I making excuses for this monster? It still doesn't negate the fact that he'd killed some of his own men, taken me from the court to his room, and he's kept me here since.

"You were saying?" His fingers drum next to his plate. Fingers with clean-cut nails, long, lean fingers that have been inside me, that have known exactly which part of me to press against, which part to arouse and bring to climax.

My belly cramps, and I clench my thighs tighter. No, no… I can't be turned on by just thinking of everything he's done to me. And yet there is no mistaking the moisture that dampens between my thighs, that makes the shirttails stick to my underside.

He stiffens; his big shoulders bunch. His nostrils flare. The beast knows that I am turned on.

"It seems even though you are past your heat cycle your body still wants me."

"I don't."

His lips curve up in a smirk. "The sweet musk of your arousal says otherwise."

Hearing the words only turns me on further. A moan ripples up my throat, and I bite down on my lower lip to stifle it. "You shouldn't say such things aloud," I mumble, and heat flushes my cheeks.

His gaze widens. He watches me from under hooded eyelashes.

A spurt of heat tugs at my lower belly and I look away. I can't meet his eyes, not without giving away how much I am feeling right now. And it's lust, only lust.

The cord trembles against my rib cage, unfurling, sending a pulse of such need shooting down to my core. "Ah hell!" I huff out a breath.

There's a low chuckle from him.

Bet if I look up I'll see a smirk tugging at his lips. The one that draws attention to his mouth, that makes me want to rake my fingers through his hair and drag his face down to nestle between my legs. I squeeze my thighs together. "It can't go on like this."

"Like what?"

"Like every time we have a conversation or if we are in the same space, there is this need to…to…"

"Fuck?" His voice is rough.

Sweat beads my palms. My toes curl. I squeeze my eyes shut, and try to block the sight of him from my head. That only heightens my other senses. My skin tightens. The hair on my forearms rise.

I sense his big body shift. Feel the heat roll off him and know he's crouched down in front of me. His legs brush mine and I try to slide back in my seat, but he only shifts his bulk in synchrony with me.

"Oh, what the hell are you playing at?" My eyelids fly open. Mistake. He's so close now, too close. He's within touching distance. The skin around his eyes tightens. A pulse tics at his temples. That complex woodsy scent of his bleeds into the air. Images of his hands on me, his lips on my mouth, of how hard he felt inside me. How good. How right. All of it crashes over me.

The force of his personality is a living breathing thing in the room. It pushes down on my chest, squeezing my rib cage. My shoulders hunch. "Don't." My voice breaks. That familiar ball of emotion is heavy in my throat. "Not like this." I ball my fingers into fists. My lips tremble.

His gaze falls to my mouth. His breath grows rougher.

He leans in close and the heat from his body slams into me. Dense clouds of warmth swirl over me, and sweat breaks out on my brow. Then, as I think that he's going to pull me up—or worse…or better still, drag me to the floor, push aside my shirt, and take me right there—he moves.

## 28

Zeus

I am so close to her that I can see the little creases around her eyes. I can see the pores on her skin, the freckles on her nose, the creamy expanse of her throat; I want to lean in and touch to remind myself she is as soft as I remember her to be. Then her throat moves as she swallows. Nervousness and fear come off her in waves.

And that stops me.

When I had dragged her here and fucked her… It wasn't completely against her will, for she had all but begged me to take her, but she was also in the high of her heat cycle then, had not been in her right mind, and her body had needed me. But now?

Her gaze is clear even as those green eyes burn with desire. Her body trembles. The sugary scent of her arousal fills the air. She presses her bare toes into the floor. Every part of her is eager for me, and yet she holds back.

"Don't be afraid."

She starts at my voice, her gaze flying to my face.

Her pupils have dilated again. She is more aroused than she realizes. A yearning flows to me down the mating bond.

It tugs at me, pleads with me to take her, yet I sense a resistance. A reluctance to give herself to me. I could overpower her and take her... but... No. I rise to my feet so fast that she gasps and pulls back into the chair. And she's not meek—at the height of her heat cycle she fought me, she wanted me, but didn't want to give in to me. It was only when the hormones had overridden every other part of her rational mind had she asked me to take her.

I feel a grudging respect for that, though I shouldn't.

I know then that I can't stop at seducing her into giving me what I want, and that only turns me on even more.

The hardness of my arousal strains against my pants. Yeah, like her, my body, too, has a mind of its own. Given a choice, I'd drag her to my bed, and then proceed to mate with her over and over again until I'd marked her completely. I'd own her such that she'll never again refuse me, that she'll never again be scared of me.

Why is it so important that she comes to me of her own accord? That she wants me as much as I want her? That she accepts the mating bond?

"How long can you resist?" I take a step back.

She stares. Color rushes to her cheeks. She swallows. "You will be surprised. Remember, I was a virgin all these years. I managed to see through many heat cycles on my own, without asking the first alpha to cross my path to take me."

"And yet you did." I smirk, my lips pulling up at the sides. I sound like I am gloating, and I am. It is the truth, after all. "You did ask me to take you. The alpha who rescued you from a room full of marauders."

"And yet, you weren't careful with me either." Her hand flies to the shredded, still-healing marks on the side of her neck.

I angle my head and survey my handiwork. Satisfaction curves my lips up in a smile. "No. I mated you."

"Why?" She shoves back her hair so the strands float around her shoulders. "You could have rutted me through the heat cycle, could have taken all you wanted from me and then let me go."

"But you see that wasn't my plan."

"You didn't know who I was then, did you?" Her body stills, and she stares at me

"I didn't," I agree and lean back on my heels. When did this entire conversation change tack? Why is it that she always refuses to follow my lead?

With my men, I tell them what to do, and they bow and scrape to please me. They follow my command.

Except Ethan who has a mind of his own. Which is why I respect him…which is why my admiration for her ticks up a notch. "You are no ordinary omega, Lucia."

"Lucy." She folds her arms over her chest and thrusts out her chin in a gesture I am beginning to recognize.

"You know why I brought you here, Lucy. I intend to keep you here for as long as it takes."

"As long as what…?" Her lips tremble.

I want to go to her and soothe her, and yet a part of me says if I do that I'll be lost. That I'll give her the power if I do so, and then what? Would that be so bad?

I pace.

When I'd mated her, my only thought was that she was mine, that she belonged to me.

What I hadn't counted on was for the mating bond to go both ways. That I belong to her as much as she does to me.

And I want to tell her that, but something in me refuses.

I can't.

I am here in this palace for one reason only. To destroy the legacy of the man who had shown my mother no mercy.

Her gaze bores into me.

The tension grows in the room, filling the space, mixed with that edge of sexual need that always seems to be there between us. That will never go away no matter how many times I mate her.

"Answer me," she says, her voice low but firm.

"I intend to keep you here for as long as it takes for you to acknowledge who I am."

"Who are you?"

"Your mate."

## 29

Lucy

I hear his voice as if from a distance. See his face set in an expression of determination. His jaw firms. A nerve ticks at his temple.

His chest planes ripple under his dark skin, and all I can think of is going to him, dragging my fingernails over his chest and marking him. Then, throwing myself at him and asking him to take me over and over again until I reach that space where all that remains is that bare essence of my soul—a naked need, a burning desire to be part of something.

To be joined to him in a way that I have never been to anyone else and never will be again. And that thought is a shock.

But is it, is it really? When I'd known from the time I'd set foot in this palace that there would be only one logical conclusion. That I was going to be taken and knotted, and not by any alpha, but by the most powerful of all of them. And inside I'd been ready. More than ready. Maybe it was that genetic superiority in me that came from being part of the royal family of Russia that expected to only be united with a bloodline that was different from the norm.

Which was what my father had intended for me, with the alliance he had forged with the leader of the Vikings. I had turned my back on that and run away…straight to a fate that was apparently not very different.

"Why me? Why choose me as your mate?" A shudder of nervousness runs down my spine. The hair on my neck prickles and stands up. It shouldn't be important to hear his answer. It shouldn't matter what his reasons were to bond with me. And yet it is. Something primal inside me insists that I force him to admit what I'd already sensed. "Tell me." I hold his glowing blue gaze.

A myriad of expressions flit across his face. For a second, I sense that vulnerability that I thought I'd touched, that I'd felt when he was deep inside me, when he'd insisted that I say his name.

It is then that I realize that behind that charade he projects to the world he is as lonely as me…and I am sure he is going to finally tell me something that is real, that matters.

Something that will give me a reason to push aside everything else that binds me to the outside world and gives me the space to finally be myself, to accept the bond that tugs and pulls at my gut and is worming its way into my soul.

He straightens his spine.

His shoulders stiffen.

His features form into a mask of indifference. Once more he is the General, the leader of the insurgents, the alpha who killed his own father and took over.

"Because I need a mate by my side, to win the respect of my followers. To show the old guard that I am serious in my claim to being their leader. To cement my position of power."

"So it is to further your own needs?"

"Obviously." He angles his head.

His gaze narrows and he searches my face. Does he expect me to react with surprise? Or perhaps he wants to see some other emotion; one that will set right everything that has happened.

"No." I gulp. Is all of this a ploy for progeny? My palms fly to my belly, and I want to tear them away and tuck them at my sides; but I don't.

"Yes." His voice is soft but firm. "I want to control, command, dominate and use you."

My nerve endings stretch. My core trembles, and I fight the need to cover myself. To throw myself at him and ask him to follow through on his words.

Then, "I want to touch you, hold you, kiss you, and protect you." He frowns as if his words puzzle him. "To keep you safe so that someday you may carry my child." His gaze drops to my stomach and stays there.

His voice cuts through the thoughts skittering in my head. A child. Someone of my own. Someone born of my own flesh and blood. It pulls at that nurturer I've hidden deep inside of myself, that I've tried to drown out all of these years under the voice of rebelliousness, under the need to be independent.

And I am still all of that.

Only, I am also an omega. A fierce provider, someone who was born to procreate. And the thought doesn't fill me with horror. Not even the fact that it is this monster…this alpha who could have already impregnated me, and that he'd done it without sharing his intentions with me. That he'd done it in a cold, calculated manner. All of it…he'd planned all of it. I sink against the back of the chair. "You'd been looking for an omega for this reason."

"Not any omega, but one of superior breeding to ensure my future generations can weather everything that the future is going to bring. Imagine my surprise when you sweep right into my clutches? One sniff of your scent and I knew your genes were exemplary. Learning that you came from the royal family of Russia only sweetened the deal further. And, of course, then there is your cunt." His gaze slides down to the apex of my thighs.

I resist the urge to squeeze my legs shut. Try to pretend that hearing him talk about that part of me is not making my flesh weep with need. That his gaze sweeping over me does not encourage moisture to trickle from my core.

"Your sweet pussy that made it abundantly clear that it ached for me." He raises his gaze to my face.

Those molten eyes deepen until they seem to be almost clear pools of spring water.

A mirror in which I can see myself reflected.

One that I want to shatter, but which I know is going to tear me apart instead. My stomach twists.

"I don't want you." I force myself to keep my features straight, to keep all emotions from showing on my face. To clamp down on the lust that pushes at me and thumps at my temples. "I don't want you…" I shake my head. "I don't."

"So you keep saying."

His jaw firms, and I am sure he is going to close the distance between us and take me and throw me on the bed and bury himself in me. And I want him, too…with every fiber of my being. I tense my body, grip my forearms so my nails dig into my skin. My toes scrunch into the floor, and I wait…and…he swivels on his heels and stalks to the door.

I watch, not sure what's happening.

A part of me already aches that he is leaving. While my core throbs with unfulfilled lust and my lower belly pulses with readiness, my mind says this is the right thing, that he did not force himself on me. That he did not seduce me to give in to him. There's a ball of emotion in my chest that's growing larger by the second. The breath shudders out of me.

He pauses with his fingers on the door handle.

Every part of me tenses up again.

He turns and fixes that glorious blue gaze on me. "When you face up to the fact that this is not one-sided, that you want me, that you need me to break you, that you revel in it, that more than that, you are but this…an omega who wants every depraved thing that only me, only your alpha, can give you. That only I, Zeus, can fulfill you. When you finally accept that and ask me to rut you…only then will I mate you again." He shoves open the door, which slams shut behind him.

# 30

Zeus

I'd walked out of there and that was not what I had intended. I'd wanted to try to be civil, to stay with her, make sure she was okay after the last few days. And that thought itself is so unnatural. What does it matter how she feels? She is my hostage. The daughter of an enemy who'd walked into my palace with the express need to hurt me. Why did she agree to do that?

I'd never bothered to ask her of her intentions.

I didn't need to.

The look on her face when I had called her out on her own identity was proof enough. Besides, I am judge, jury, and executioner. I don't need to explain my decisions to anyone, and certainly not to an omega.

And yet that part of me that seems to come alive when I'm around her, insists that I give her the benefit of the doubt.

Why is it that the sight of her green eyes, wide and with tears shimmering in them, haunts me? That scent of hers, that familiar, honeyed, sugary essence clings to my every pore, tugging at my nerves, while the mating cord in my chest thrums with discomfort.

A feeling of sadness seeps through the bond. She is hurt and lonely, my omega.

Well, she deserves it. Doesn't she? She'd known what she was getting into when she'd flounced into my lair. Surely, she hadn't thought I'd go easy on her. She couldn't have possibly known that I'd spare her...and yet something inside me insists I should have treated her with care.

That I should have asked her first, given her a chance to defend herself. Right... Next, I'll be asking her permission before I mate her. I have already done that...in a sense. I'd told her I was going to wait until she came to me. That until she really wants me, I won't take her again. Fuck this! I am losing my mind and all over a timid omega, over a pair of green eyes that haunt my soul, over a sweet cunt that grasps my shaft and milks it as if it has been designed for me. Whose womb throbs in readiness, and I know that she is the one who is meant to birth my offspring. Did I just think that? Am I am waxing poetic about her...? Do I still have my balls? No fucking way am I letting a female get the better of me.

Striding out of the palace into the courtyard, I stop at where my troops are practicing.

"So our mighty leader arrives," the hulking alpha lurking in the corner of the courtyard drawls. "I take it you found the omega satisfactory? Given we haven't seen you here for a few days. Most unlike you, mighty Zeus, the Bastard of the East End."

I swerve toward him.

Jerome sniggers, then the fool saunters out into the center of the court to stop in front of me. "Yet by the glowering darkness on your face it seems perhaps she is not to your satisfaction? Care to pass her over perhaps? Maybe what she needs is a real male to satisfy her."

Blood thunders in my temples, and red sparks flash in front of my eyes. My fingers twitch, and the next second, I find myself hauling Jerome up in the air, his legs suspended off the ground. A fight is exactly what I need, and this...this sniveling excuse for a man will do quite nicely for getting his head pounded into the wall.

I stalk toward the wall, carrying him along with me, then slam his head against the hard surface, again and again.

Blood sprays out, and bits of his flesh fall to the ground.

There is the sickening sound of his skull cracking, but I don't stop. All I can think of is no one dares talk about her like that in front of me. No one dare look at her again. "She is mine," I roar. "Mine." I slam the man's head into the wall with such force that it flattens all the way down to his neck. His body grows limp, and I throw the irritating burden to the side. Turning, I pound my chest. "Anyone else?"

The soldiers have formed a wide circle around me. On their faces I see fear, desperation, also resignation. What's missing is respect. What I've craved from the beginning.

The need to redeem myself in front of the people who've made me their leader.

I've wanted this, craved this power since I was five and had caught a glimpse of my father sparring with his troops right here in this courtyard. And yet every time I'd tried to live up to his expectations, tried to live up to my own dreams, I have failed. The only thing left for me is to destroy this town and show them once and for all who is the most powerful alpha.

No one meets my gaze, except Solomon who stands there, eyes narrowed, a look of understanding on his face. I glance away.

Ethan steps forward. "Want to take on someone your own size, Alpha?"

"You have a death wish, Second?" I crack my neck from side to side. Truth is, that's exactly what I need. A chance to pit my skills against someone who can hold his own, who will challenge me, push me, take my mind off the annoying, beautiful, alluring woman whose thoughts send a pulse of desire shooting to my groin. Yet who I've sworn not to touch, not until she asks for me to take her.

Ethan's lips pull up in the semblance of a smile. He has his armor on already. He holds up his sword and takes position.

My gaze falls to it. "Barehanded. No weapons."

The color slides from his face. A nerve ticks at his temple.

He is unsure of how he'll fare against me without his favorite weapon. Good. When I was running wild on the streets of the East End, I had no access to fine weapons. All I had were my wits and my bare fists. Fighting freehand is what I still excel at. No one has defeated me, ever. Many have tried and been hurt.

The same thoughts must have run through Ethan's mind, for he nods and hands his sword to Solomon.

He shrugs off his armor and lets it fall to the ground.

I take off my vest and fling it aside.

We walk to the center of the courtyard and face each other.

The heat of the morning sun pours over us. People begin to stream onto the balconies above us.

I bend my knees, raise my fists, and am about to charge forward, when a soldier runs into the courtyard.

"The omega. She's gone."

# 31

Lucy

The shirt I wear, *his* shirt, whips around my thighs. Reaching the other end of the building, I hear the shouts as soldiers pursue me.

I still can't believe he'd left the suite without locking it behind him, that there had been no guard on duty. Zeus was crude and an alpha-hole, but he wasn't sloppy. Had he done this deliberately?

Yet, this is too good an opportunity, and I have to take it, even if it means being caught and punished. I have nothing to lose.

The sound of footsteps racing in pursuit thunders, and blood thuds at my temples; my pulse beats so fast that I feel dizzy, yet I keep going.

I run through the gardens, to where the scent of the river floats to me. A cry breaks out behind me, and I pick up my pace.

My feet skid on the stones, and pain rips up my legs. I bite my lip to hold back my groans. Stumbling over the uneven ground I reach the parapet wall and peer over the side. The water of the Thames churns below.

My heart pounds. A chuckle rips out. I thought I was so clever to escape. Thought I would be brave enough to jump and leave the alpha behind.

The mating bond in my chest throbs and a shudder of desire races down my spine. My throat closes. No. No. This is not happening. I cannot be bonded so closely to him that he can anticipate my fears, my uncertainty, even predict what I am going to do next. Once more I glance over the parapet at the river.

My head swims, and a moan emerges from my mouth.

I grab the platform of the parapet. Can I do it? Can I take this final step? Or am I forever fated to be here, bonded to a man I know nothing about? Who knows my identity? Who probably suspects that I had an ulterior motive to have come this far? He'd found out my real identity but he still doesn't know the real reason I am here. This is my chance. This.

My heart stutters. The mating bond pushes against my chest. He's coming, he is. I don't need to look over my shoulder to sense his presence.

"Lucia."

His voice shivers over my skin. The mating bond stretches and pulls at me to turn around. I squeeze my eyes shut.

"Don't…don't come closer or…" Pain floods down the mating bond.

The fear that comes down the connection almost blinds me. It also confuses me. He can't be afraid for me. He doesn't care for me. But he'd walked away from me that morning and given me a choice. In this instant I know I've made a mistake. I've found the one person who finally recognizes what I am inside. Not any omega. Not a meek female. Not only a submissive. Someone who is his equal. Someone he won't treat as another breeder, but one who he'll want to please. He'd grabbed me from that room full of alphas, but he'd actually saved me from them. He'd taken me for himself, yet each time he'd also made sure to pleasure me. And his touch… his feel…his caresses. Desire tugs my groin, and slick gathers and drips from my core.

"I am not going anywhere, Lucia."

Another pulse of heat trickles down the bond. There's a yearning there. A need to fulfill, to take care of me that I had refused to accept. And now? It's too late, it is. I turn to him.

"But I am." I smile at him. Tears prick my eyes.

"Wait." He flings out his hand and closes the distance between us.

I push back against the wall. The breath catches in my throat. My hands slide on the parapet, and then I am falling, falling. I think I scream, but I am not sure. The wind gushes past me so fiercely, so strong that my eardrums seem to rupture. Then there is only silence and pain that rips through me as I hit the surface of the water and sink under.

# 32

Zeus

"No!" My heart slams against my rib cage, and I race toward the parapet. I throw my leg over the wall, but arms seize me and yank me back. "Let me go," I roar at the intruder.

I scan the river, searching for her. There is only the churning, swirling mass of water that is the treacherous surface of the Thames.

I can't see her.

There's no sign of her.

Another pulse of worry twists my guts. My stomach lurches, and my breath comes out in pants. My vision narrows. The hair on my skin pops. I grab the arms that restrain me and rip them off of me, then leap for the wall and jump over the side.

Keeping my arms close to my body, I hit the water and go through. Opening my eyes underwater, I look for her. Nothing. I don't see anything. There is a ball of fire in my chest, squeezing my heart. I fall inside myself and reach for the mating bond and find it quiet.

So quiet.

Fear shudders down my spine. Surfacing up for another gulp of air, I then dive below, my gaze scanning the space. And again. My arms are so tired, legs so heavy I find the current overpowering me. Know I must swim to the riverbank, else I'll likely drown, too.

Closing my eyes, I reach for the bond and stretch my consciousness out through it, searching, sensing, and all I find is white.

A silent whiteness so blank it could be a canvas that will never be painted on.

My guts twist, my stomach churns, but I can't give up. How can I when the one thing that brought the color into my life is gone? Darkness closes in on me, the water tugs me down, and I try to push back, knowing I can't give in to the tiredness, cannot let myself fall.

Everything I've faced to come this far seems to hit me. Images of my father, my mother…my followers, the need to destroy the city…all of it is chased away, and all there is, is her.

The sugary scent of her slick, the softness of her skin, the brilliant green of her eyes when she is aroused, the fear that rippled through her, the first time I'd seen her, her fighting me…submitting to me… The mating cord twinges, once, so faint I should have missed it except I've been waiting, waiting for that.

My eyelids fly open, and I aim for the faint light that filters through the waves, sinking through the green depths, the color so like her eyes. I am going to see again. I will see her safe, I will find her, rescue her, bring her back, and when I do, I am never letting her go. Never again. I push back strongly and rise to the surface. When I break through, my lungs expand, and I draw in huge gulps of air.

"Zeus."

I look to the other side to see Ethan waiting for me.

It was him who'd tried to hold me back from jumping; no one else would have dared. Only he has the guts to face me, and I want to rage at him for trying to hold me back. Yet, when he wades out to grab my arm and hauls me to the shore, I don't shake him off.

I am too tired, too overwrought, too anguished to think of anything else but her.

Reaching land, I keep walking, Ethan at my heels.

He touches my shoulder. "We'll find her, Z."

I stiffen, then jerk my chin.

Notice I don't admonish him for reassuring me. Me? The alpha who's never needed reassurances, who'd never have accepted comfort from another, hell, who'd never have revealed his vulnerabilities to himself let alone the world—that alpha; he's the man I used to be. I set my jaw and stalk forward. I am changing and there's not a damned thing I can do about it. It's her fault. The damned omega is softening me up. I'd almost flung myself into the river without caring for my life. I've never put myself on the line for anyone else, for no one except my mother. "Alert the troops, send out search parties, alert the guards along the river."

"Now you insult me."

I turn and narrow my eyes at him. "Fucking Second," I snarl without heat. "Always one step ahead of me."

He meets my gaze. "Of course, you'll want to be part of the search party and head out yourself?"

I angle my head, not bothering to reply.

When I reach the bridge leading away from the palace, Solomon is already there with my armor.

I shrug into my suit. "Put out a reward."

"Already done—"

"A million quid."

There's silence. I shoot him a sideways glance, "Stop trying to second-guess me...*Second*." I peel my lips back at Ethan.

His lips firm. "Of course, your omega is worth that and more."

"Another million if she is found unwounded. I want her unhurt, if so much as a hair on her head is touched I'll set waste to this city, you understand?"

His features are frozen, all the expression wiped off his face.

He's going to protest that we are stretching our already lean financial resources to find a woman, I wait for him to say it, just so I can pick a fight with him, put him in his place. One excuse that's all I am gonna need to lay into this motherfucker. My fists clench.

Ethan's gaze narrows, then he angles his head, "Of course, General."

Bloody fucking hell! It seems I don't need to explain to him exactly how much she's come to mean to me.

Reaching the bridge, I slide into the armored car which Sol has brought around for me.

"She could be dead…" Ethan gets in the front next to me.

Sol takes the back seat.

I snarl, "She isn't." I start the armored vehicle and roar up the bridge.

"How do you know?" Ethan scratches his chin. "Ah, the mating bond."

"You can sense her?" Solomon leans forward.

I shoot him a glance in the rearview mirror and he pales, then folds his arms over his chest.

Ethan turns to me, "You know what this means, right?" His voice is quiet.

"I am sure you are going to tell me," I grit my teeth.

I shouldn't allow this degree of familiarity from him, but whatever.

We are going to search for her, and yet the fact that we are under so much pressure has brought down any walls there may have been between us.

There's silence in the car.

When it has continued long enough, I curl my lips. "Say it fucking already."

"It means"—he pauses for effect and turns to Sol—"he is aware of her through the bond. He can track her through the connection. It also means if one of them dies—"

I set my jaw. "The other dies, too."

# 33

Lucy

I wake up with a gasp, sitting up so fast that the world spins around me. I am not sure where I am. The bed is rough under me, not as rough as some of the places I've slept, but different to the silks of the bed that I'd become accustomed to over the last few days…or is it weeks?

In Zeus' stronghold, I'd lost track of time, and suddenly I can't wait to see the outside world. One look…one glance to see where I am, enough to get my bearings. I swing my legs over, and when my feet touch the floor a pain shoots up my legs. My guts churn, and bending over, I try to retch, managing only to dry heave.

Footsteps thud toward me, and before I can straighten, hands grasp my shoulders, holding me as I cough.

The acidic taste of bile is in my nose, crowding in on my throat, and I rest my forehead against my knees.

I feel lifeless, like everything in me has been brushed out, like every part of me has been broken and then put back together again, only whatever has been formed now is something different, a body with which I am not quite familiar. I feel…discombobulated. Where did that word come from? My English tutor who had taught me and my sisters in Russia, who'd been from here, from London. Her accent had been so different to his.

"Zeus." I breathe out his name, and the sound of my voice echoes hollowly in my ears.

The person holding me urges me to sit up. Soft hands pull back the hair from my face. A pair of warm brown eyes peer into mine. "You need to lie back, you are hurt, and your feet are not in great shape," the woman says.

I glance down and wince. My feet are dirty, toenails dark around the corners. I don't need to look at the underside to know they are scratched and bruised.

There's blood smeared on the floor.

The scent of copper is suddenly too intense for me. My stomach twists; my chest heaves. "I am going to be sick again."

The woman nods and springs up, dragging me up with her. She pulls me along to the bathroom. Every step I take hurts, but I'd rather bear the pain than be sick all over the floor.

The bathroom tiles are cool under my feet, and then I am doubled over the ceramic bowl in the corner.

I hold on to the rim and puke until it feels as if I've coughed up every single thing I've eaten in the last week. By the time I collapse back onto the floor, sweat beads my forehead. My chest heaves, and I can't feel my legs or my hands for that matter.

A cold towel is pressed to my forehead, and I moan my appreciation. She holds it there with one hand, then offers me a glass of water. I try to take it from her, but my hands are shaking so much the water splashes all over the long shirt I have on. The mating bond coiled against my rib cage throbs, sending a pulse of pain shooting down my spine. I rub the skin over my chest. My gaze darts to the woman.

"You're bonded to an alpha." It's a statement, not a question.

I frown. "How can you tell?"

She jerks her chin toward the wound on the side of my neck. Only then do I become aware that it's bleeding again. My entire side screams with pain, and there are splotches of blood over the cloth covering my chest. "A shower. I need a shower."

"You are too weak — "

"Please." I let the glass slide from my fingers so it falls to the floor and rolls away. Reaching out, I grasp her arm.

She tosses her dark-brown hair over her shoulder. Her jaw hardens, and those warm eyes glow with understanding. "Let's get you up."

She rises and helps me to my feet.

She's taller than me. Muscles weave across her arms. She's wearing dark pants and a shirt. There's a whiff of dominance around her that marks her out as alpha…almost.

Except she isn't. The delicate features of her face, her soft touch as she staggers with me to the shower, the fact that she took me in… The concern that rolls off her says she must be omega.

"How?" I force the word through a throat that feels that it's been sliced with knives.

"How do I manage to survive as an omega in a city full of alphas gone rogue?" One side of her lips twists. "We have much to catch up on…but first." She helps me into the shower, turns on the warm water.

Then assists me in taking off my shirt and props me up. She proceeds to bathe the mating wound which has softened and oozes pus and blood under the hot water. By the time she helps me back into the bedroom and helps me pull on a T-shirt and drawstring pajama bottoms, I am shivering and hot at the same time.

My chest hurts. The mating cord whines and throbs, and there is a pounding at the back of my eyes that feels like it's going to rip through my brain.

I don't protest as she half carries me to her bed and shoves me under the covers.

The bed smells of that strange alpha-omega confluence. How the hell had she managed that? Most omegas yearn, to be born a beta, or better still an alpha or at least find a way to hide their smell. While this woman hasn't completely succeeded, her scent is confusing enough to buy precious seconds by throwing an alpha off track. Enough to give you time to escape in a struggle. A few seconds, that was all it took for him to capture me; to make me his.

She tugs the blankets all the way up to my chin. "Sleep, recover, and we'll talk more about what brought you here and how we can help each other."

Something at the edge of my consciousness prickles at that. "Help each other? How can we?" I mumble.

She runs a cloth that smells of something fragrant, something that slides into my blood, calming the mating bond. Darkness tugs at the edges of my vision and I slide under.

When I wake again, there is a man in the room. "Zeus?" I crack open my eyelids.

The shape moves. The light shines over his face, a lean face so handsome it's unmistakable.

Indigo eyes glow at me. So familiar, yet different. His lips pull back in a smile that is so pleasant it coerces you to trust him. I am not fooled.

He's the predator here in this room, but I am done with being prey.

I try to rise, and the room spins around me. My heart thuds against my rib cage. This can't be happening. I didn't just escape one alpha only to be cornered by another.

The same woman who'd taken care of me earlier moves to stand next to him. "You promised you wouldn't shake her composure, brother."

"Brother?" I groan out the word, then swallow down the dryness in my throat and ask the question I should have asked earlier. "Who...who are you?"

Silly, trusting me.

I'd never stopped believing in the kindness of strangers. I'd simply accepted her help, and now here I am facing the biggest enemy of all. Kayden. Alpha of the Scots.

He rises to his feet. He's almost as tall as Zeus.

I'll always measure any man I meet against the prowess of my own alpha.

*My* alpha? Where did that thought come from? Why do I still think of him as mine?

I try to sit up, but my arms can't take my weight. The woman who hasn't yet told me her name sits on the bed and supports me. I pull away from her, but my movements are weak.

"I'm sorry I had to drug you, but it was the only way to make sure that you'd stay."

"And I thought I could trust you."

"It was for your own good, I promise, Lucy."

"Who are you? How do you know my name?"

"Reena Kane. I am Kayden's sister."

"You called him here?" I cough. My pulse thuds in my temples. How do I evade Kayden? Assuming I did manage to escape, where would I go?

By now Zeus has alerted his troops and is no doubt searching for me. He may already be on his way to the city. My mating cord twinges and unfurls, insisting that Zeus won't do me any harm.

Why would my very consciousness already be one with him?

Why does my instinct tell me to trust him…more than the man sitting opposite me?

The man who'd promised to help me, who'd sheltered my family?

"Where are the other omegas?" I focus my gaze on him, ignoring the way his figure weaves in and out of the picture in front of me.

"They are safe and waiting for you."

"Safe?" I chuckle and cough again.

Reena rubs my back, and once more I try to sidle away from her. She lets me move out of her grasp, and I fall back against the pillows. My shoulders shake with the effort, and sweat beads my brow.

"Well, by the looks of what happened, they are safer where they are at any rate." Kayden takes a step forward.

The alpha scent of his presence grates on my nerves. This is not the man I want. This presence is foreign, intrusive. It is hurtful to me, to what I could one day carry inside of me.

My throat closes.

Zeus had wanted to impregnate me.Could that have happened already? The mating cord thrums with emotions, and tears well up in my eyes. There's passion and joy and a need to survive that ebbs and flows inside me. I've never felt like this before. Helpless and yet also hopeful.

Knowing he will come to me.

If I let him find me, I won't be able to resist him. I'd let him take me again and again, and I'd enjoy every second of it even as I hate myself. It's inevitable that I fall pregnant if I am not already.

I cannot let an alpha who took advantage of my heat cycle to bond with me, also plant his seed in me.

I will not let any child of mine grow up in the shadow of the man who is so confused he doesn't even know himself.

I must not let him near me again.

The mating cord pulses against my rib cage, insisting that I am wrong. But I shove it aside.

"Kayden." I push back on the bed and this time sit up without any help. "Why are you here?"

"Isn't that obvious? You want the safety of the omegas. I want this city."

"Isn't there any other way but to kill Zeus?" The moment the words are out, I know it's a mistake.

Kayden's features form into a mask. He's so good at hiding his emotions; his face is inscrutable. Unlike Zeus, who as much as he tries to keep his feelings under control, I can always sense them lying there under the surface. Waiting for me, calling to me, aching...for me. The mating cord whines and shivers. A shudder runs down my body.

"You are bonded to him." Kayden angles his head. "You care for him."

My breath catches in my chest. I want to deny it, but from the silence in the room, the way that Kayden stares at me, the way Reena moves away from me, her nostrils flaring as she sniffs me, the realization that Kayden is right dawns on her face, and I know it's too late.

"So it is him? He is the alpha you are bonded to." Reena wrings her fingers together, and in this moment it's clear she is much more omega than alpha.

"Are you going to give me up to him?" I glance from Reena to Kayden.

His lips peel back in a smile. "Give you up? Hell no." He stalks to the seat and slides back into it, legs parted, chest planes wide, hands gripping the arms of the chair and dwarfing it. "You are bait, sweetheart. The alpha is hunting his mate, and when he gets to you, guess who will be waiting for him?"

# 34

Zeus

I wake up with my heart pounding. Sweat drips down my back so my vest is stuck to it. There is a feeling of impending darkness, of something so heavy in my chest that it seems to get larger by the minute.

I swing my legs over the side of the bed and stay there, panting. My heart stutters, and I rub my chest.

The beats are erratic. There is a sense of impending gloom. Of something coming at me, something more sinister than anything I've faced before. I hang my head forward, grip my knees, and will myself to breathe. One breath, two breaths, slowly, in and out. Focus, I must focus. The mating cord in my chest strains and a groan rips out of me.

My scalp prickles and I wipe my damp palms on the sheet covering the bed. I know it's her emotions I am feeling. She's afraid.

When I'd taken her, I had only meant to bind her to me. My only thought had been to ensure that I had someone who belonged to me. Not to the city, not to my men…not to the sense of duty that despite everything I do, I carry with me.

Perhaps I am my father's son more than I'd known. Perhaps hidden somewhere inside is this need to do right by the city, and I don't understand where it is coming from.

This sudden attack of conscience that's forcing me awake in the middle of the night.

This need to keep my omega safe.

My Lucia…it is because of her that I am being tainted. Her thoughts, her emotions, her idealistic need to do good by all, it's dripping into me. Creeping in my subconscious. The mating cord binds her to me, but it also ties me to her. It's influencing me in ways I cannot begin to understand.

Fear shudders down my spine, and helplessness…and mixed with it is this urgency. Is she trying to get to me, to warn me away?

My shoulders bunch.

I raise my head, firm my thighs, and push myself up on my feet. I walk out of the door of the bedroom in the warehouse that I've kept in the city. Another relic of my father's days. He'd kept this house incognito in order to be able to go about the city without being recognized.

One of the traditions that I decided to continue.

I stagger into the living room to find Ethan walking in from the other room.

Solomon, who's been keeping watch in a chair by the window, rises to his feet. "What are the two of you doing up? It's only four a.m." He yawns and scratches his chin.

"I need to go to her." I strive to keep my voice low, but it comes out harsh. I shake my head. I have to find a way to control myself. Whatever is happening to me, there's an easy explanation for it. It's normal, isn't it, when an omega is bonded to an alpha, to be aware of her emotions, to perhaps also want to take care of her?

I squeeze the bridge of my nose. Where are these thoughts coming from?

"You okay?" Ethan's voice cuts through the thoughts swirling around in my head.

"Why wouldn't I be?" I snarl out, angrier with myself for feeling this vulnerable.

It's as if the mating cord is burrowing inside my soul and ripping out all the layers I've built over the years. It's laying my emotions bare, making me feel naked and exposed, and I don't like it. Not one bit.

Walking to the table next to the surveillance equipment that Sol had been monitoring, I pick up the bottle of water and drink from it.

It does nothing to soothe the sick feeling twisting my stomach.

Pouring the rest of the water over my head, I then drop the bottle back on the table. "What's the latest? Have any of the soldiers seen anything?"

The mating cord throbs and a wave of terror engulfs me. My skin seems to burn, and there's a ball of emotion in my chest so huge that I cannot breathe.

I stumble to the window, and grabbing the sill, I shove open the pane and lean out.

It's a security risk to do that. Anyone could recognize me…which is not the issue. My own citizens aren't exactly filled with love for me. Not like I've done much to deserve their respect either. And fuck…there I go, playing the violin again.

I've never, in all these years, thought of their needs even once, about what I can do for them.

My father had done his version of the right thing. He'd flung my mother back to the East End of the city, the gutters where she'd come from.

He could have kept her, taken care of her and his son, but he hadn't cared. Not for her, not for any of the omegas. He'd only cared about his precious city…well, for the parts that are filled with the upper classes, the rich and wealthy who live in the districts closest to the palace. He'd made sure they had everything they needed. He'd turned his back on the poor. And me?

I'd gone a step further.

I'd wanted to punish the ruling classes but I'd ended up doing my worst by both the rich and the poor. It didn't matter what your class, or your status or indeed where you lived. I was an asshole to everyone alike. Everyone except her. With her, I cannot keep up this charade; it has always been nothing but a front.

Just, I've never wanted to own up to it. I cannot let her do this to me.

Being near her, in her, having her essence mixing with mine is changing me from the inside out. It's making me…more empathetic, wanting to do good for my people, but this stinking city has given me nothing but fear and pain and a start in life that I'll never be able to live down. I cannot allow myself to develop a conscience, not now.

I cannot let myself care for my people.

Cannot let the man I really am come to the surface. The one who feels duty-bound to do right by his city.

The one who wants to use his power to change the flawed system that my father had so callously imposed.

I've come too far.

Planned too long.

Lost too much.

Too much to let one omega sweep in and upset all my plans, to change me, mold me into a version who is half me...the real me who is a responsible, conscientious leader who wants to protect his people.

The kind who, no doubt, the fucking history books will love to sing about...no, that isn't me.

I am a monster, an illegitimate bastard who took great pleasure in using his power for one thing. The downfall of the bloodline that had given birth to him and given him nothing else. Nothing. This city is going to Hell. And I am going to be responsible for it. That's how I want the future to remember me.

And I intend to live up to my reputation.

Starting with her.

I am going to find her and teach her a lesson, the kind that will ensure she never dares face up to me, never dares run away from me again. The little princess of royal blood is going to be broken completely by the most nefarious bastard in all the land. Me!

The mating cord in my chest thrums and pushes against my chest, warning me I am wrong. Telling me not to do this. Pleading with me to reconsider. Nah. No way can a simple bond do that. So what if it links me to her?

So what if I am using the connection to find her. It is only a means to chain her to me. To bond her to me for now. Forever. So no one else can have her. No one except me. That's all it means.

That. Is. It.

I turn to Ethan. "It's time to move."

# 35

Lucy

I walk to the window and look out over the grimy city.

The buildings are all low, a relic of the past when government laws decreed that no construction would be tall enough to block the view of the parliament building from anywhere.

The same structure that the monster now uses as his base.

The same monster who had taken me, rutted me and broke my heat cycle. A trickle of slick dampens my core. I squeeze my thighs together.

He is still a monster.

He may have not fucked me against my will, still, he had taken advantage in the midst of a heat cycle when I had been desperate for any alpha's touch.

No, not any alpha...but him.

I push the thought away.

He hadn't given me a choice. He hadn't restrained himself. But then...I hadn't wanted him to either. So why are my thoughts still on him?

Why does every part of me want to go to him, to feel his touch on me, his wide palm gripping my hips as he brings me closer and lowers me down on his shaft, and again… A moan is torn out of me. There has to be a way out. I can rip the bond from my chest, break this connection so he won't be drawn to me as I am to him.

So I won't imagine that he is already somewhere in this city, getting closer, closer, closer to me.

Wanting me, missing me, yearning for me as much as I am for him.

The mating cord thrums and gnaws at me, tugs at my nerves and stretches, pushes into my chest.

My spine curves and my eyelids fly open.

My breath is coming out in gasps, and my heart is racing. Fast, so fast. My chest thrusts out, and I feel like I am being pushed forward to the tips of my feet, yanked out of my body. My very soul is fluttering inside, slamming against my skin as if my very essence wants to pour itself through the cord to him. Him. No! I curl my fingers into a fist and slam it on the wall. Pain flutters over my skin, but the wall doesn't crack.

Of course not.

Physically I am still an omega.

Still weak.

I may be fast on my feet, quick with my thoughts, know how to use my intelligence and my beauty to seduce, but I'll never be as powerful as an alpha. Did I really think I could break out of here? Out of the prison that another alpha had imposed on me?

It isn't fair that omegas have to always depend on someone else; wherever you turn, there is always someone bigger, more powerful, one step ahead of you. Someone strong enough to do the things you want to do. To reach the heights you want. Who takes what you need. I always feel like I am lacking, as if I am secondary, and the world would rather I give in, roll over, and submit…except when I am with him.

Oh, make no mistake, he wants me to submit to him…and I want him to make me. A shudder of fear laced with desire tightens my stomach. Can he sense that I am I thinking of him? Am I drawing more attention to myself? Calling him to me? I stand there yearning for him, hating myself for it, yet unable to stop the shudder of pleasure that runs down to my core. My stomach cramps in anticipation, yearning for that deep, rich fullness that only an alpha, *only he* can fill.

That feeling of utter completion that I'd felt only once when he'd covered my body with his and slammed into me again and again; that feeling of oneness as he'd bitten me and the pain had swept through me, pushing away all other thoughts except that it was me…and him…and I was his. Irrevocably, completely, fully his.

He is the monster; I am his victim. And yet he owns me, and not against my will. And that is the sad truth. Only with Zeus do I feel like I am something, that I am at the center of his world.

The city may hate him or love him. Either way, they want a piece of him.

Yet with him…I am his world.

He may deny it, may not acknowledge it, perhaps abhor the idea, but the fact that he wanted me, needed me…enough to have mated me.

The mating bond tugs and whines in my chest, yanking me forward with such force that my spine curves again.

My chest thrusts out, and my spine curves. A force that I cannot see urges me to keep going. I fling open the windowpane, shove my leg over the sill, and begin to slide forward to the muddy ground three floors below. All the time my gaze is still on the palace in the distance, across the river.

The site of my mating.

By knotting me, had he bound me not only to his body but also to his soul, to that very place where he had taken my virginity? And what will I do when I find him again? Ask him to take me back? To forgive me, and then what? I sit here, legs dangling, thoughts buzzing in my head, my vision narrowing, focusing. My thighs firm, my shoulders bunch, and I lean forward when arms grab me around my waist and yank me back. No, no, no. I fight against the restraints, rake my nails over the barriers that hold me back. I push, wriggle, bring down my head and bite, and kick out.

"Let me go, please." I hyperventilate.

"No." Reena's voice whips through my ears.

The strength in her grasp digs into my waist, and the ground recedes.

Another strong pull and I fall back into the room, to the floor. I hit my side and the breath whooshes out of me. All thoughts spill from my mind. Pain shudders through me, and I focus on that. The mating cord writhes in my chest and I hate the damned thing. Loathe it.

How can something unseen control me like that?

I am not a coward. I've never thought of taking my life no matter how rough things were in the past. And I hadn't meant to put myself in danger, not like that, and yet when I'd seen his palace, all that had mattered was that I get out of there and go to him and find him…and he wasn't even there.

The cord pushes me to get to my feet. The hair on the back of my neck rises. Every instinct tells me to get out of here and find him. I don't question how, but I know where I must go. It's the only way out.

If I want to salvage anything of myself, if I want to retain my own identity, then I need to put enough of a distance between us. I must slam down a barrier that separates me from him before his essence bleeds through me and mingles with my thoughts and I don't know who he is and who I am; before we become the kind of bonded pair that not even death can part, I know what I have to do.

I stop struggling and let my body go lax. My shoulders hunch, and I let my muscles loosen.

Reena exhales a breath. She pulls her arms from around me and moves away, pushing herself to sit. "What were you thinking?"

Her voice is disturbed and angry, and yet I also hear genuine concern. She is Kayden's sister, a man I now know I can't trust, and yet Reena is like him but also not.

She's the one who asked him not to hurt me, who tried to hold him back. And Kayden, it seems, respected her wishes and left right after that meeting. I haven't seen him since. Is that good? Or bad? Where is he? What is he scheming about now? I am not quite sure, to be honest.

I am relieved that he isn't around. It seems wrong to be in the presence of any other male, any other alpha except the one who is my own.

Except he isn't…my own.

He belongs to no one — not to me, not to this city.

The mating cord shudders and cringes inside my chest. I rub the skin over it. It shouldn't hurt so much to think of him.

To feel him flow through my blood as if his essence is already inside and mingling with mine. It should scare me to realize that I am sensing his thoughts, that I am seeing him more clearly than anyone else has. A deep loneliness bleeds down the bond, and uncertainty, and fear…so much fear. About his past, his future, about losing me. I shouldn't feel it. I don't want to feel it. It's not right. I shouldn't feel this close to a man, a monster who took me when I was at my most vulnerable, the one who bonded me before I had a say in the matter. He used my heat cycle, my need to be physically rutted through the cycle against me...a man who used my vulnerability to claim me?

Can I trust him?

Can I allow myself to see the sliver of genuine goodness I sensed somewhere deep inside him?

More than that... It is a strength, a passion, a fierce will to follow his heart, to do what is right. Except what he feels is right is not always right for the world. And I am the only one who can see it, feel it, sense it deeper than he ever has. What am I going to do about it?

Should I allow myself to draw him out, let Kayden capture him? Do I have a choice? If I don't, Kayden will kill my clan. Yet, if I lead Kayden to Zeus, if I allow Zeus to walk into the trap, Kayden will kill him, and as one half of a mated pair, my days will be numbered. Either way, only one thing is certain—I am going to die.

A calm descends over me.

That is right. A peace, an end to this existence which has become so twisted and convoluted, so entwined with the life of another who I have no desire to call my own. To whom I am becoming more attached with every passing moment.

If I kill myself first...? It is only a matter of time before Zeus dies, too.

Kayden will get what he wants. And my clan will be safe.

The more I think about it, the more I know this is the only way out. The mating cord curls on itself and anguish pours from it. Fear pounds through it, slamming into the presence at the other end, and I know Zeus can sense I have decided on a course of action.

He doesn't know what it is, but he knows already that he does not like it.

I sense his will flood down the bond. Sense him pulse reassurance, heat, a lick of fire...enough desire for my nerve endings to flare, to cramp my womb, my core moistening with need. He's not holding back, Zeus. He's trying everything possible to change my mind...from what, he can't know, but it's as if he's thrusting the very force of his will, his dominance on me to stop me from what I am doing.

Sweat breaks out on my forehead.

At the same time, moisture laces my core.

My heart pounds so fast I am sure it is going to burst out of my rib cage at any moment.

A breath wheezes out of me; my lungs seem to be unable to take in any more oxygen. Every part of my will resists Zeus' influence, even as my body insists I go to him. That I am half of him. I am nothing without him.

"No," I scream and slam my fist on the floor. The skin over my knuckles breaks, and the smell of copper is in the air. I let the pain center me.

"What is it?" Reena's voice sounds over me. She grips my arms and tries to hold me down.

"Help me," I gasp out.

The world whirls around me.

My vision wavers. If I don't see Zeus soon, feel him, scent him, lick him, and draw of him, I am going to be reduced to a blubbering mass of need that nothing and no one can fulfill. This is not what I want. Not to be bonded to someone who feels so close that they are a part of me...even as my mind, my very will, that primal, rational thinking part of me still resists. The fight is going to kill me anyway...if I let it. I didn't choose how to come into this world, but I am going to choose how to end my life...in a way that benefits those I love the most. My family.

Reena's face fills my vision. Her chin trembles, and her grip on my arms firms. "Tell me what you need."

# 36

Zeus

I race out and onto the streets I'd traversed as a child. The safe house is in the East End of the city. I am sure this is where my father met my mother. Neither of them mentioned it to me, but the thud of my heart, the heavy feeling in my chest, and that sinking hole in my gut confirm to me this is where the two of them had run into each other. This is where my father took her for the first time. For all I know he fucked her in the very house, in the bed where I had lain at night. My gut churns, and leaning over, I puke. I've never done this before, been so affected by the thought of my parents, been so tuned in to the plight of my mother.

I cared for my mother, protected her from hoodlums in the neighborhood when I came of age...but had always consciously blocked out all thought of how it could have been for them to be together. How it was for her to have run into him, to be attracted to him, to submit to him knowing all along he was never going to recognize her. A whore from the wrong side of town, who survived the wildness of the streets. She had enough courage to face up to the alpha who wouldn't let go of her, not until he'd had his fill of her…and yet she hadn't been able to protect her heart from him.

She'd fallen for my father, the General, had been taken in by his fine clothes, his power, his charisma, and had submitted to him. Golan never gave her the recognition she deserved. He'd never taken her for a mate, not officially.

I realize now that my mother must have begun to affect him, too. He must not have realized how much the mating bond goes both ways. He'd thought with her death he'd be rid of her influence. He hadn't bargained on how much her death would shorten his lifespan, too. He'd gotten progressively sicker, weaker after her death, and when it came to killing him, I'd eschewed the weapons and used the ways of the street.

The mighty Golan, killed by old-fashioned strangulation. Oh! The irony. I chuckle.

This scent of blood is heavy in the air, and the reek of poverty is all around me. The stench of desperation and helplessness that permeated my childhood clings to my skin, twists my insides. And I have had enough. I need to get out of here.

Pulse pounding in my temples, I swing into the armored car and set off. Sol and Ethan are following me separately. Ethan had insisted on that, and I know he is right. I owe my second a lot, not only for thinking on his feet but also for agreeing to me embarking on this harebrained mission on my own.

He'd known there was no way out.

He'd sensed how much the bond was affecting me.

He'd gleaned how much she meant to me.

And he hadn't said anything, not made a fuss, not protested. Had stepped up to the role I need of him. To agree, yet watch out for me.

Yeah, he is one smart motherfucker, and I am never going to let him know that. I am never going to share with him how much his actions and that of Sol's in following us, no questions asked, have made me feel like the lowest heel ever. I had only questioned, resisted, pushed them at every turn. Yet they are loyal to me.

Loyalty. An alien concept, that I still refuse to accept. Unlike her. The only thing I believe in is her.

I am going to get to her and claim her all over again, but it isn't for the reasons Ethan thinks. It isn't because I can't live without her. Not because every cell in my body throbs for her, not because the mating bond yanks me forward, showing me the way, unerring in its direction as it leads me through the twisting alleys, onto the broken expressways of a once proud city, and away from London... Where is she? A few miles of driving, and I smell the sea. She is headed to Dover? Why? Is she planning to leave this city? Take a ship somewhere?

My heart stutters.

My guts twist.

I press my foot on the accelerator, and the vehicle leaps ahead, almost colliding with a slow-moving caravan. I swerve around it and keep going, knowing it is going to take Ethan and Sol longer to catch up in whatever mode of transport they have decided on. Nothing is as fast as my custom-made truck, my one insistence...almost a compulsion, this need for speed and control. And dominance. Everything that had come together in one perfect pattern when I had claimed her. I hadn't thought then. I had ridden that rush, that feeling when I was inside her when her soft core had clamped its moist heat around me, tugged me in... It had been like coming home.

"Fuck." I slam the wheel with my fist and step on the accelerator. The tires squeal, and the hated countryside streams by, still green despite the fact that the rains have been failing over the years and the weather has gotten more erratic. Too hot one day, snow the other, an unpredictability that has reduced lifespans and altered genes, all in one generation. Enough for humans to be divided into alphas, betas, and the rarer omegas.

Enough for me to realize that I was meant to be the strongest alpha of them all, from the time I had taken on the beasts who had tried to rape my mother and killed them. Then sealed my future when I had taken over as General of the city.

Enough to be sure that I have to get to this omega before she does something she will regret. I will make her regret it. And I am looking forward to it.

I plan to wrap those glistening strands of her hair around my fist, yank back her head to reveal the expanse of her neck, then sink my teeth into the claiming mark to reaffirm my ownership.

The mating bond screeches with need, and fear pours down it. The heaviness in my chest is so big, so cold, I know she is in danger. I need to get to her.

My chest thrusts forward, and my breath comes in pants. The force inside me grows larger, pushing out, shoving against my rib cage. It propels me forward. To keep going and get to her before it's too late.

I veer off the road, onto the muddy path leading uphill, then that, too, fades. I keep going, through the mud and faded grass, onto the flat plateau that soars up to a cliff.

The wheels churn, and the truck's tires strain for purchase. I brake to a stop and jump out of the vehicle, not caring that the truck begins to roll back. I can't retrace my steps. I don't care about what I've left behind. My heart stutters, stops, then ratchets up in speed. The mating cord urges me on, farther, faster, keep going. Now.

I reach the first peak and then I see her.

Poised ahead, at the top of the second peak of the cliff right ahead. Around her the white chalky surface gleams a dull creamy silver. So like her skin…no, her skin is softer, richer, smoother.

Waves of fear pour down the mating bond, so intense, so strong, that they threaten to overwhelm my senses. My breath comes in heaving pants.

Sweat pours down into my eyes. Still I push forward. When I am not ten feet from her, she turns.

Her long hair gleams with hidden golden highlights, red in the fading sunshine. Suddenly I can't wait to discover everything about her. Her secrets. Her lies. Her truths. Her fears and innermost desires. I want it all.

She angles her head at me. "You shouldn't have come."

"I couldn't stay away." I slow my steps.

"You should leave."

"Not without you." I come to a halt not five feet from her.

"Go." She raises her chin.

I chuckle, and there's nothing happy about the sound. It's twisted, yearning, full of fear and anger. At her. At me. At this damn city that brought me to this place. Facing the woman who is becoming more important to me by the second, who I'd taken without mercy, who I haven't yet broken, who I know I am going to own, and not only because she is my mate…well, maybe that, too, but really, it's because I want to.

Because no one can stop me.

She throws her head back and laughs.

No one except her.

My heart stutters.

I know what she is going to do, even before she takes a step back.

Even before she has swiveled to face the open sea.

"No!" I leap toward her, close the distance between us, and grab her hand.

My fingers touch her skin and slide off.

Then she is falling, falling.

I keep going and dive off over the edge of the cliff.

To FIND OUT WHAT HAPPENS NEXT GET *CLAIMED BY THE ALPHA, KNOTTED OMEGA 2, HERE*

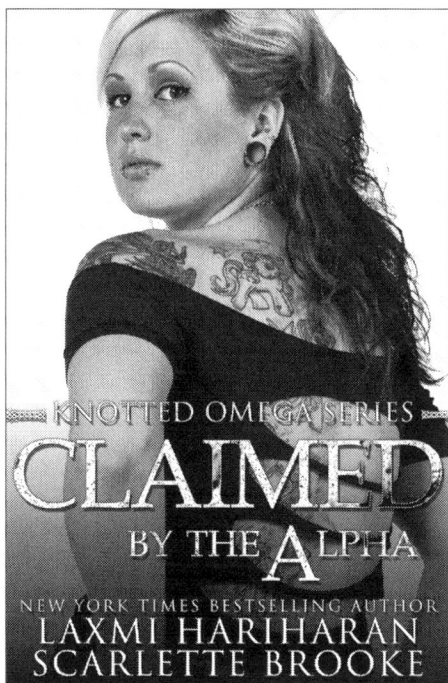

Read an excerpt...

Lucy

When I come to, it's to the sense of heat enfolding me. I burrow into the warmth, the hard planes of the chest that shift under my cheek. The scent of fresh rainwater on parched earth fills my nose.

That alluring, growing need curls in my belly and my core trembles. Every instinct tells me I am safe.

Safe?

I try to move and find there is a heavy arm around my waist, its weight both brutal and soft.

The friction of his skin over mine sends a tremor of heat down my spine.

Slick pools between my legs. My stomach cramps, and the mating bond in my chest pulses with life. Heat. Life. Energy. My scalp stings, my fingers and toes tingle.

Every part of me prickles like it's coming back to life. Like I have been asleep for a long time. Like I'd never jumped off the cliff and straight into that blue-green water, hitting the waves, going through and—my eyelids snap open.

I am surrounded by his smooth, honey-brown skin, which is broken by the scars on his throat, the wounds I had marked him with. They bleed into the tattoos on his chest.

I reach out and trace my fingers over those swirls and curves, those colors that are as stark as the monster I'd thought him to be, as poignant as the lost boy I had glimpsed in his eyes in the seconds before I'd jumped off the cliff and into the sea below.

Why had I done that?

Willfully sent myself to a possible death, while deep inside I'd known it wasn't going to happen that way? That I'd just started living. I'd just met him, and I wasn't going to let go of him or the future I'd glimpsed.

Had I been testing myself? To see if I was as brave, as fearless as I'd thought myself to be? To test him to see if he'd come after me? And he had.

The thoughts tumble around in my head. There is a fluttering in my stomach, and I push against his chest.

A growl rumbles from him. "You're awake?"

"Where am I—?" My voice cracks; my tongue sticks to the roof of my mouth.

When was the last time I drank water?

Well, if you don't count the gallons I swallowed as I sank under the waves, eh? A chuckle wheezes out of me.

I feel lightheaded, enough to be able to laugh at this strange scene which might well be from a dream. Except it isn't. The man-mountain moving under me, his flesh surrounding me, the pulse of need flooding down the bond...all of it tells me I am alive. "Why did you save me?"

He doesn't reply at once.

Is he considering his words before speaking? Strange. The Zeus who'd taken me like it was his due had never given thought to the feelings of another.

He cups my cheek, and his touch is so gentle, so sweet. "You didn't leave me a choice, little squirrel."

My throat closes. That term of endearment...does it mean that he cares for me? Nah. Not possible. So why does it feel like I betrayed him when I ran from him? He took me without giving me a choice, I was right to leave him.

"It won't work, you know." His voice reverberates under my cheek, so growly and yet so soothing.

I want to close my eyes, burrow into him, merge with him, and go right back to sleep.

"What?" I swallow, somehow knowing what he is alluding to, but that isn't possible. He cannot read my thoughts, can he?

"You keep trying to leave, not realizing that I will follow you."

His words send a wave of need coiling through my womb.

What the hell is wrong with me?

"I will always find you, and claim you." His jaw tics, and a nerve throbs at his temple. "You are mine to own. To claim. To possess."

The passion shimmers in the air between us.

The hair on my neck prickles. The flood of raw emotions, of fear and lust and his utter need to take, flows down the bond. My chest hurts. The back of my eyeballs begins to throb.

It's not like he doesn't know every inch of my body, or how my flesh responds to him, not like he hasn't shown me how much he wants to dominate me. He wants to break me.

His gaze narrows; the skin stretches over his cheeks.

My chest grows heavy. There is a ball of emotion inside clawing, waiting to get out. The force of it is bigger than the mating bond, more profound than the physical urge to want him to rut me, more primal than the need to procreate that is inherent in my omega state.

It is real, alive and writhing inside of me, and that scares me.

This need to tell him that I am his.

To respond to that call of his mate, to tell him I am here for him, that he can take me, slake his thirst in me, bury himself inside me, and knot me all over again. And I want it all. So much.

The depth of my emotions washes over me and floods into the bond, sweeping through it.

Under me, his heartbeat increases in speed. Heat pours from his chest, and his muscles go rock-hard. Can he sense what I don't dare tell him? That I hadn't meant for it to be this way?

Why is it that he just has to look at me, touch me, hold me, and I will dissolve, shatter into a million pieces, each of which reflects his name? Screams this monster's status. Alpha. My alpha. Mine.

The mating bond curls inside me, tugging at me, yanking at me, pleading, urging, begging me to accept.

"No." I yank myself from his hold with such speed that I must have taken him by surprise.

His grip loosens, and I wriggle out from under his grasp. Hitting the hard floor, I push myself to a standing position. The world swings around me. His big body moves. His muscles tense, and he springs up to his feet, arms outstretched to catch me.

My legs tremble, and I punch my toes into the floor for support. "Stay away…" I gasp.

I don't need to ask him to know that he saved my life.

I lurch to the door and shove it open, stepping onto the fine white sand. There is a beach in front of me, sloping down, ringed with coconut palms, and beyond that the sea, waves, and the blinding sun shining off of it for as far as I can see. It should be idyllic but it is not.

It should gladden me that I am away from the smoggy, dirty streets of London, but it doesn't.

I am here alone with him. My skin puckers.

I stumble forward and onto the beach. My feet sink into the sand. I look down and draw my gaze up the curve of my ankles, to my legs, over my bare thighs, to my stomach. My breasts are bared to the sun.

I am naked.

Heat flushes my cheeks. All this time, in his arms, I didn't have any clothes on.

Something sounds behind me, and I swing around and flush. Blood rushes to my cheeks, and I know my neck must have turned an interesting shade of scarlet. For the man is naked, too.

He has not a stitch of clothing on.

Not his pants or those massive boots I've seen him in. Nope. There's a vast expanse of honey-brown skin, marked with those tattoos I'd been admiring down to the sculpted planes of his stomach, and below that his shaft, which is already semi-erect.

"Wh...why did you bring me here? Why did you rescue me?" Why am I bothering to ask him this question?

He confirms my fears. "One guess?"

"Uh, because you needed time away, and this is your island retreat?" I swallow.

"Wrong answer." His stance is patient. He's waiting, waiting.

"And because I am your..." I squeeze my eyes shut.

"Say it." His voice is soft.

"Your..." I force myself to open my eyes. "Omega."

"And?" He takes a step forward.

I hold my place. I will not be scared. I am not going to step back. Not going to show him how afraid I am. That my heart is pounding, my throat is dry, while sweat breaks out on my forehead. "And I need water. I am parched."

He turns and walks inside the house, then reappears at the door with a bottle of water.

A bottle?

So someone has stocked this place. I lean back and take a better look at it. The structure is rudimentary but seems secure. It must be for Zeus to bring me here. Why is it that I trust this alpha so implicitly with my safety? Was it because he'd jumped into the ocean after me and saved me?

I want to ask him why he did it but I am not sure I want to know his answer. Not least because I don't want to question the warmth that pools in my chest at the thought of him risking his life for me. My captor had become my savior and how do I feel about that, eh? Why am I not panicking? My toes curl and my fingers and toes tingle. With fear? Anticipation? Both?

I close the distance between us and snatch up the bottle, "This place belongs to you?" I gulp down the water then hand the bottle back to him.

Without wiping the top, he tilts it to his lips and chugs down from it, too.

It feels very intimate. My lips tremble. I want his mouth on me again. Longing sears my belly, and I push back the need to press my thighs together. But I must have given something away, for his gaze drops right back to my core.

He bends to place the bottle at the side, on the ground, then straightens. "It's just you and me, and no one is going to come here, not until your lesson is complete."

"Lesson?"

"Yes, little omega. The one you need to learn." He looks at me. Hooded eyelids. The silver in his irises is as liquid as the sea behind me. As tempting as the water, I had dived into when I had jumped off the cliff. There's a pleasure-pain of calling in them. They scare me and seduce me at the same time.

"Which one is that?" I dig my toes into the sand.

"You want me to spell it out for you, little squirrel?" His lips thin. His nostrils flare.

That threat in his tone sets my nerves jangling.

I know what he means. And it should terrify me. Should warn me to stay away from him.

Still, that spirit of disobedience that has brought me this far, that has gotten me into trouble so many times, urges me not to cooperate with him. Not when I am so clearly in his control. "I have no idea what you mean."

He closes the distance between us so quickly that I gasp.

He grabs my nape and pulls me close. His fingers are long enough to curl around my neck all the way so his fingers meet in the front.

My pulse rate ratchets up.

He lowers his face and his nose bumps mine. His eyes narrow, and his jaw goes solid. The scent of dominance leaps off him, so thick and fast that it plows into my chest. Sweat breaks out on my forehead.

He rubs his thumb over the front of my neck. "Perhaps I should show you what happens to omegas who run away from their mates."

My breath hitches; anticipation tugs at my belly, and moisture beads my core. Why does the brutality in his voice turn me on so much? Why do I want every depraved thing that he can do to me? It should feel wrong and it doesn't.

I can't stop myself from pressing my thighs together to hold in the moisture that threatens to leak out from my core. I need to put an end to the hold he has on me. I must.

"You are not my mate." The skin over my heart ripples. The bond pulls at me, scolding me for not accepting what I already know.

"You are right."

"I am?" I stare.

"I let you out of my sight. I left you before the ending of your heat cycle, when you needed me, instead of consolidating the bond." He pauses, surveying me, watching me, stalking me like the prey I am.

And I am tired, so tired of being on the defensive with him.

Mates aren't supposed to trap you or drive you out of your mind with need until you yearn for their touch, then deprive you.

Mates who are alphas are supposed to hold you, rut you through your heat cycle, then cherish you and bring you down from the high, none of which he has done.

A pulse ticks at his jaw. "I am going to set that right." He steps forward and cups my face.

"No." I shake my head. "I don't want that…I don't."

Swooping down, he places his forehead on mine and purrs, a low, glorious resonance that is drawn up from the depths of his core. The notes ripple up his massive chest with such strength that the vibrations thrum over my breasts.

My nipples pebble and the flesh between my thighs weeps.

The sound of his purr strums my sensitized nerve endings. My core clenches and moisture gushes from between my legs to form a puddle under me.

A sob rolls up my throat. My chin wobbles and I raise my hands to his chest, wanting to push him away.

All I end up doing is spreading my palms, sensing the vibrations that throb up his ribcage. It's strangely soothing. An affirmation that he is alive. That I am still alive. I push back from him. "Why do you insist on doing that?"

He bends and scoops me up in his arms then walks back toward the house. "You like it when I purr." His forehead furrows. "It brings out the need inside you. Speaks to the omega essence of you."

"Exactly!" I peer up from between my eyelashes. Those piercing blue eyes of his deepen in color. Mistake. Why am I trying to reason with him when all he has to do is look at me and I want to fling myself at him and ask him to take me all over again? "That's why I don't want you to do it." I shove my hair over my shoulders. "It's difficult to think, let alone speak when you do that, and then it leads to the inevitable."

He steps over the threshold. My gaze flies past him to the narrow bed at the far end of the room.

There is barely enough space for one person. An image of me curled up against his broad back, my face pressed into those sculpted planes washes over me. It's both arousing and reassuring, and the mix of emotions confuses me.

I shouldn't be so needy for him.

And it's not just my body.

My will is melting along with the rest of me, getting used to his presence in my head, in my heart, in every part of me which has begun to recognize his flavor and thirst for it.

His essence flowing down the mating bond is bending me to his will. I drop my head.

I have been fighting this attraction to him for so long. My shoulders slump. I lower my chin toward my chest, and my hair spills over my face.

"So what would you rather do?" His voice reverberates up his chest.

My insides quiver. Why is it that as I am trying to be logical, my body is hyper-aware of him? I huff out a breath. "I just want us to have a conversation without any distraction."

He crosses the floor toward the bed. "Okay."

"Huh?" I blink, staring up at that impenetrable visage. Whatever it was

I expected, it wasn't for the devil to agree to my request. "So you'll be willing to answer a few questions first?"

"One." He sets his jaw.

"Three." Guess there is some use of having grown up in a royal household and eavesdropping on discussions my father had with his Council. All those negotiations, all that give and take I've witnessed is ingrained in my blood.

"Two." He straightens his shoulders, and I sense he's back to being the General again. He also doesn't seem very surprised that I'd tried to talk him up.

"Okay," I agree before he changes his mind.

"Hmm." There's a low exhale of breath from him, then he lays me on the bed. Pulling up a chair, he flips it around and goes to straddle it.

"Wait." I spring up on my knees.

"Now what?" he growls, his massive shoulders flexing as he folds his arms over his chest.

"You may be used to being naked, but I am not." I jerk my chin at his body, not daring to lower my eyes to that chest. If I do, I'll be lost. If I look down to where his shaft is growing harder by the second, I have no doubt I'll close the distance, grab it, lick it, and then lower myself onto it...and... not yet. I squeeze my eyes shut. "Let's put on some clothes. Please, just until we have this conversation."

He turns and stalks away.

I blink.

Not what I'd expected, okay? I mean, this here is an overbearing alpha-hole, the monster who runs this city as if it is his personal dictatorship and...maybe I misjudged him.

I push the thought away. Nah. Being this close to him, sensing his warmth, the tug of the mating bond, all of it is skewing my judgment. Next, I'll be thinking of playing happy families with him, of him and me and our children in his stronghold. I shake my head to clear it.

Clearly, I am losing it, and the worst part is, none of it seems wrong.

It feels natural, more organic than anything I've ever felt before. How can it be a mistake, when all my instincts scream that it's right?

"Give an omega an inch, and of course she's going to take over your whole damned life." He strides to the closet I'd glimpsed in the corner.

It's so unexpected. The General of the city, the alpha of alphas, muttering under his breath like he is a henpecked man. I giggle.

He shrugs into a pair of loose linen pants. He stalks back to me and flings a tunic at me. It's big enough to cover me all the way to my knees and smells of the sea.

I slide it on then plop down on the bed. "You've used this place before?"

He angles his head. "Even a bastard like me needs a retreat, somewhere to get away and clear my head."

"You mean regroup on the assholeness inside so you can go back and be more of a bastard?" Oh, hell, there I go again, inciting him. Why can't I just stay quiet? Why can't I conform to the stereotypes of omegas? Gentle. Docile. Right. So not what I am.

He frowns. A nerve ticks above his jaw.

My pulse thuds at my temples, but I hold his gaze. So, the guy's a monster. No argument there. Still, he's been less of a jerk than I'd thought. He rutted me, gave me what I needed, saved me…from the stupid-ass attempt at trying to drown myself, and now he's actually trying to have a conversation with me?

Everything I've always expected from someone normal. Someone who isn't a monster inside. Which he isn't. And I have never wanted someone average, normal…have I? That would bore me.

And here I go making excuses for his behavior again. I rub my palm over my face.

Walking back to the chair, he straddles it. Then smirks in that way I am beginning to think of as The Zeus Special. "Yeah, that's exactly right. And I'm done being patient. You get one more question, Omega. You'd better make it count."

*To find out what happens next get **CLAIMED BY THE ALPHA, KNOTTED OMEGA 2, HERE***

*"One heck of a primal read, this alpha is a sex god." -USA Today bestselling author, Lee Savino*

*Love bad boy alpha-holes? Look no further…*
*The sexy Dark Fae of the FAE CORPS, are the heroes of the Fae's*

CLAIM SERIES.

"★ ★ ★ ★ ★READING THIS BOOK IS LIKE BURNING IN FLAMES OF PASSION, LUST, AND DANGER. A TURBULENT RACE TO AN EXPLOSIVE CLIMAX." AMAZON TOP 250 BESTSELLING AUTHOR SKYE JONES

READ AN EXCERPT FROM DANTE AND GIA'S STORY

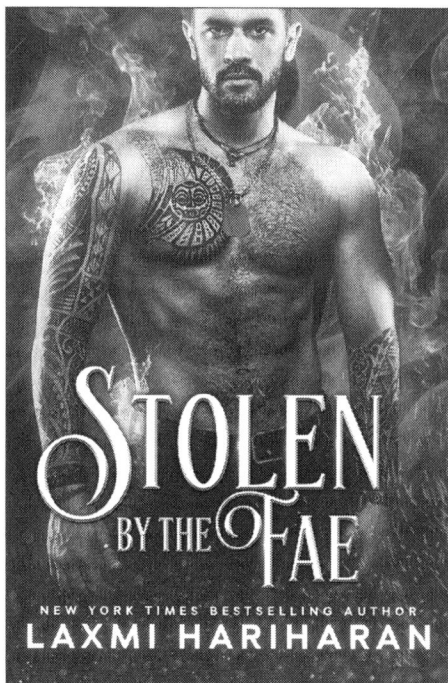

Gia

"Incoming heat missile." The bartender stares past me.

I turn, and he clicks his tongue. "Don't be that obvious."

Right. I bite the inside of my cheek, then straighten to peek in the mirror above him.

A group of men talking, two women conversing at the far end. Everything seems normal. Exactly why I'd chosen this watering hole at the edge of Red Square in Moscow.

Then, one of the women points to the entrance of the bar.

I follow her gaze.

The figure of a man fills the doorway. He's tall enough for his head to graze the top of the frame.

The hair on the nape of my neck rises.

Sunlight pours over him, and his features are in shadow. Yet there's no mistaking the sense of danger that radiates from him.

The bartender lowers his voice. "Good luck."

I grip the bottle of water, the skin over my knuckles stretching tight. "What do you mean?" I swig from the liquid, wishing it were something stronger. But I can't afford that, not when I have to return to duty with the Bureau of Shifters later today.

"Alpha-hole headed your way." He chuckles.

"Wait. What?" Every instinct in me snaps to attention.

He jerks his chin in the direction over my shoulder, then moves away.

Don't look, not now. I hold my breath. Then heat slams into my back. It's as if a furnace has been switched on behind me.

My mouth goes dry.

The scent of the first rain on parched earth teases my nostrils. My blood thumps.

I raise the bottle of water to my lips again, when arms cage me in on either side.

I peer out of the corner of my eye and see a corded forearm peppered with dark hair.

Muscles flex under the tanned skin and flow down to meet long, tapered fingers.

Hands that could trail over my skin, grasp my curves, squeeze my flesh, and massage them and... Heat flares in that secret place between my legs. I clench my thighs.

A flutter of lust licks my belly.

I lower the bottle. My fingers tremble, and my palms go slick with sweat.

I swivel around on the barstool and stare at the widest pair of shoulders I have ever seen. The man is massive; his big body blocks out the sight of the rest of the bar.

He doesn't move. Just stays, hunched over me. He's all around me.

His perfectly sculpted pecs are accentuated by a plain white T-shirt that clings lovingly to every single muscle. Dog tags nestle between those hard planes, and his nipples are outlined against the fabric.

My mouth goes dry.

I want to lean in and lick the valley between those chiseled planes, then drag my tongue over his skin, across to that nipple and bite it.

I swallow and raise my eyes.

The tendons of his beautiful throat flex as I move my gaze up to his square jaw. There's a shadow of a dent in the center of his chin. My fingers twitch. I want to reach up and trace the furrow.

One side of lips turns up in a smirk.

Bet he knew exactly what I was thinking just then.

A shiver runs down my spine and my nerve endings stretch with antici-pation. He won't be gentle, this man. He'll take without regret, and... I want him to do just that. I want to nip on his pouty lower lip, then swipe my tongue over his cruel mouth... A mouth made for snarling, for suck-ing... for taking... Heat sweeps my skin.

I tilt my head back, and farther back, forcing my gaze to climb over that hooked nose to the furrow between those hooded eyebrows and... I gulp. Blue eyes blaze at me.

They are turquoise and sea blue with a hint of green, and there are amber flecks that ebb and flow in them. It's as if there's a fire that's lit inside, one which is reflected in those irises. Yet his pupils are so dark. Empty. Cold. So cold. A shiver ripples down my spine and... whoa! Is it possible for one pair of eyes to have so many conflicting emotions?

This man could rip me apart and not care. He would own me, possess me, make me scream with pain, he'd bring me so much pleasure. Damn!

My thighs clench. My fingers tremble, and the bottle of water slips from my grasp.

I keep waiting for the crash of the bottle hitting the floor, except this gorgeous, otherworldly, heat-inducing, moisture-drawing, perfectly beau-tiful hunk of a guy swoops down and catches it.

His muscles uncoil as he straightens. Every move of his seems to be etched in sheer poetry. I try to move, and it's as if my body is weighed down.

He raises the bottle and holds it right in front of my nose. "Yours?"

"Mine." I force the word out through a throat that feels it's lined with shredded glass. Does he realize that I am staking my claim on him already with that word? "Impressive catch." I jut out my chin.

"I know." His voice is low and husky and tugs at my nerve endings.

There's no mistaking the innuendo in his tone. He's so damn self-assured, so confident of the impact of his nearness on me. It should annoy me, but the truth is that his arrogance is a turn-on. Sheer charisma oozes from his every pore, threatening to overpower me with the dominance of his personality.

My belly flutters. Heat flushes my cheeks. I reach out and grab the bottle from him.

One side of his lips quirk.

A kind of know-it-all, I-know-the-effect-I-am-having-on-you kind of smirk. The kind of smile that does not quite reach his eyes. The kind that promises that lurking just under the surface is a male who will take without permission.

It's bad and oh so good.

Every part of my body seems to wake up and scream for attention. For *his* attention. His very careful ministrations on every inch of my skin, my body, my soul.

Someone opens the bar door at the front. A breeze sweeps in and flows over me, bringing with it more of that fresh rain scent. It's laced with a hint of something dark. Forbidden. Out of bounds. My heart stutters.

He tilts his head. His hair is cut close to his scalp. The strands rise, spiky in the front.

I have a sudden image of my thighs framing his face as he dips his head between my legs.

My belly tightens. My pussy is instantly wet.

"You are not human," I state the obvious.

He's too well built for us to belong to the same species.

He could be a shifter... except for the way he moves, it's too smooth, too fluid, not like their more deliberate gait.

"What are you?" A ripple of apprehension slithers down my spine. And yet I can't stop staring. Can't take my gaze off that perfect face.

"Wouldn't you like to find out?" he purrs.

Goosebumps flare on my skin. I gulp. I've never had such an intense reaction to a complete stranger, not like this.

"You okay?" He peels his lips back.

It's not a smile but a declaration of intent. A promise to take without mercy. Anticipation tightens my skin. My scalp tingles.

No. "Yeah, of course. Why wouldn't I be?" I tilt the bottle to my lips and take a sip before lowering it.

Perfect white teeth flash at me, setting off that honeyed tan of his skin. That, combined with the lines that stretch from the corners of his eyes, tells me he spends a lot of time outdoors.

The man reaches out with his finger and touches the corner of my lips. "You left some behind."

Heat flickers out from that whisper of a touch, down to my core, and I stiffen. Every muscle in my body tenses.

The man brings his finger to his lip and sucks on it.

The sight of those gorgeous lips closing around his digit sends a shiver of anticipation down my spine. My belly quivers. My heart stutters. More moisture slicks my core.

What the bloody hell?

Who is this man? And why am I reacting like he is the last male I'll ever see? Probably because it is true? Because I am about to embark on the most dangerous part of my mission, and I don't want to die a virgin? Because I want to know how it is to be taken, possessed... by him? No way am I letting that happen, not by a complete stranger.

I sidle off the barstool, still holding the bottle in my hand, then duck under his arm. He lets me go and my breath comes out in a rush.

Don't turn around. Don't look at him. I stumble up the corridor. When I reach the ladies' I lunge for the door and fling it open. I cross the floor of the restroom and lurch to a stop in front of the sink.

Close call. At least I escaped.

I plop the bottle on the counter and grip the edge of the sink.

So why does it feel like I am missing out? That I'll never know how it feels to trace those biceps with my fingers, to rub my face against the rough whiskers of his chin, to have him bend me over and slam into me, and... My belly twists, my pussy clenches, and the moisture flows from between my thighs.

Heat sweeps over my skin chased by chills. Sweat beads my forehead. I don't have a choice. Looking around to make sure the space is empty, I swoop under my skirt, push aside my panties, and thrust my finger into myself.

"Ah." My groan fills the space; the sugary sweet scent of my arousal spikes the air.

I plunge the finger in and out of my dripping channel, then add another. "It's not enough." I grit my teeth.

"Maybe I can help?"

My eyes fly open, and I see his blue eyes in the mirror.

Dante

It was my presence that aroused her, so it's up to me to help her, right?

Silver eyes meet mine in the mirror. She stares at me as if she can see into my soul. Maybe she can see who I really am and why I am here?

And now I am getting fanciful.

She's only a human I happened to spot while on this mission to Moscow. Except as I had passed this bar at the edge of Red Square, I had caught the scent of orange blossoms and pepper, a spoor so irresistible that I had stepped into the bar. One look at her, and I had to have her. Just the kind of man I am. I want something, I take it. Especially curvy sprites with soft skin, and an arousal that bleeds into the air, seducing me to get closer, closer.

"Starlight." I suck in a breath. My voice echoes in that enclosed space.

"Um... what?" The heat in the space turns up a notch. A bead of sweat trickles down her temple.

I grip the ends of the basin, blocking her in. "You have stars in your eyes, and yet when I touch you"—I place my cheek next to hers— "you flinch, wanting to draw into yourself; even as every part of you blooms for me, aches for me, wants me to scoop you up and lick you all over. Everywhere, in every secret nook of yours." My heart thuds. "I want to destroy your every hole. Fulfill your every fantasy. Fill you to the brim and make you come over and over again."

Her pupils dilate.

Her cheeks flush.

I am sure she is going to run out of here screaming, or perhaps turn and slap me, either of which will only add to the pleasure. For when I have her, she will forget everything, except me. My touch, my fingers, my lips as I make her scream with pleasure. As I break her.

The witch pulls her hand out from under her skirt. She straightens, then brings her fingers to her lips and sucks on them.

Desire roars in my blood. I feel the suction of that rosebud mouth as if it isn't her fingers but my cock that she sucks.

My pulse thuds.

My shaft goes rock hard.

Whaddya know? This one is feisty. One who'd dare to go toe to toe with me. She has no idea what's in store for her. No woman has tamed me yet. And it's certainly not going to be her.

The things I want to do to her, to bring her to her knees, literally; just the thought of fucking that mouth of hers makes my balls draw up.

Only when the touch of her skin filters into my blood do I realize that I have wrapped my fingers around her wrist.

I tug on her hand, and she doesn't resist. I bring her glistening fingers to my lips and ease her forefinger inside my mouth.

The taste of her infuses my veins.

I bite down on her finger lightly, and she shivers. She wriggles her hand in my grasp, and I tighten my grip.

Coercing her hand to the side, I slap her palm down on the sink in front of her.

Her breath hitches, but she stays where she is. Impressive.

Still holding her gaze, I reach for her other palm and place it flush on the surface as well.

She gulps but doesn't say anything, just holds on to the edge of the basin with her hands. The skin stretched over her knuckles is white.

I take a step back, hold my hands up to show her I am not forcing her. I tilt my head.

She raises her chin and her lower lip quivers.

I want to tell her that now is her chance to leave. If she doesn't want this, doesn't want the pleasure I can give her, then she should get out of here. But something warns me not to speak. If I do, it will break this strange trance that holds the two of us. This communication that we have established on the unspoken level.

So I jerk my chin toward the exit, all without breaking contact with her gaze in the mirror.

Her eyes follow the direction I've indicated. She frowns, her muscles go solid, then her eyes skitter back to hold mine in the mirror.

In a very deliberate gesture, she widens her stance. She pushes back from the sink, so her butt is poised in the air. Still, without breaking the connection, she circles her hips, and again.

Each move of hers is meant to seduce. Her skirt rides up just enough so I can make out the edge of her panties. White seams, simple cotton underwear. She hadn't come here to pick up a male. She hadn't intended to part her legs like this and invite someone to glide their fingers inside her and... What the hell is this? An attack of consciousness?

"Last chance." My voice comes out on a growl. "If you want to leave, then now is the time."

Yeah, okay, so I know it's a mistake to speak, but I can't help myself. I need to share what I have in mind; and in a fashion, that leaves no room for misinterpretation.

Blame my chivalry on pure greed.

I want her to remember me with unadulterated lust. I need her to understand that she yearns for this as much as me.

Her eyes sparkle. "Who said anything about leaving?" She darts out her tongue and runs it over her upper lip.

Heat flushes my skin and sweat breaks out on my forehead.

What is it about this woman that I have such a visceral reaction to her? I've never felt this turned on, this needy for a female before. And I won't again; not for anyone else. The thought sends a skitter of awareness prickling at my nerve endings. I hesitate.

She holds my gaze in the mirror. "I want you." Her gaze scrolls down my chest to my crotch where the evidence of my arousal must clearly strain against my pants.

Even before the words have left her mouth, I close the distance between us. I shove her skirt aside, seize her panties, and tear them off.

*To find out what happens next read* DANTE AND GIA'S *passion filled* CAPTIVE ROMANCE *here*

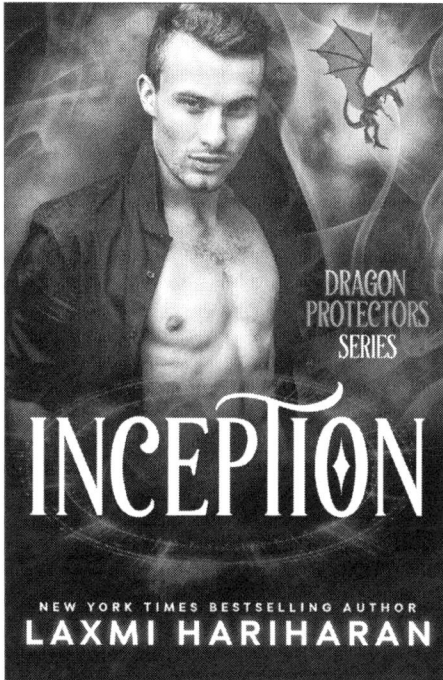

Read an excerpt...

Hope

Twenty-four hours into her break from being a sentinel of the dragons of Mauritania, Hope had walked into that bar in Bombay.

She wasn't supposed to be in Bombay.

The dragons had flown under the radar for so long. They'd kept away from people until they had all but faded from memory.

She was taking a major risk by being in that city, but she hadn't been able to resist.

The city had always called to her, and for once, Hope couldn't soothe her dragon out of the urge to visit.

A few weeks more, and she would be bonded to a fellow dragon shifter. She was looking forward to it.

Liar.

Sweat trickled down her spine. The scents of the shifters, vampires, and humans in the bar, entwined with the smell of her desperation.

She tightened her fingers around the glass. It shattered the liquid splashing onto the bar counter.

As one of the seven born to the dragon who'd founded her clan, it was her duty to mate with another dragon and continue her bloodline.

No other species could survive the psychic impact of bonding with a dragon shifter. She was screwed.

Likely, this was her last night of freedom, and she had to make the most of it.

When she was out flying through the air or winging through the seas on her boat, she could be herself. She felt free to do what she wanted, without fear of letting down her family.

It was also the reason she kept breaking the rules of her clan.

It was childish of her, but these occasional bouts of rebellion were what kept her dragon sated. Enough to allow the woman to stay in control in human form.

"Non-alcoholic ambrosia, please." She peered up at the bartender from beneath lowered eyelashes.

The man's eyebrows flew so high they disappeared under the hair that fell over his forehead. "Let me guess. You're a dragon shifter, the only species who don't like alcohol."

A jolt of fear ran through Hope. The heat of the enclosed space inside Alex's bar weighed down on her shoulders. Had she been found out?

Then she saw the teasing glint in his eyes.

She relaxed and raised her fingers to her mouth, pretending to yawn. "Do I look like a dragon shifter?"

The bartender looked over her features, down her chest, to her waist, then back. "Hmm. You're curvy and tiny and too sexy to be one."

She recognized his harmless flirting and decided to play along. "What does a dragon shifter look like, anyway?"

"Large, fire-breathing, with wings." He flapped a palm in the air. "Never seen one. They're almost extinct, right?"

"Right." She flashed a smile.

Had the satisfaction of seeing him blink.

Oh, he was interested all right, and cute and friendly. Only... she wasn't looking for any complications.

"By the way, it's not like dragon shifters don't like the occasional alcoholic drink. But when you're a fire-breather, alcohol tends to add fuel to the flames. Know what I mean?"

Hope clamped her lips shut. Hell! She shouldn't have said that. But her dragon had insisted she set the facts straight.

Dragon 1. Woman 0.

Stupid game! But it was so much more fun to keep her dragon and woman in balance this way.

Her animal was too damn close to the surface. She never had managed to rein it in. Very early, Hope had realized that unlike the others, her dragon took a lot more to control.

The bartender didn't seem to hear her muttered comment. He was too busy shaking up a concoction.

A crash from the other end of the bar had her turning that way. The hair on the back of her neck prickled. Both dragon and woman were riveted.

The clinking of the glasses, the conversation of the couple next to her... all of it faded. All she saw was him.

The man who had her attention rose to his feet, only to stumble.

She didn't even realize she was moving until she found herself next to him.

The feel of the rock-hard muscles of his shoulder bunching under her fingers sent a thrill of awareness rippling through her.

She was in so much trouble.


Aaron

Five minutes earlier

"Non-alcoholic ambrosia?" Aaron stared into his glass, hunching his shoulders. Sounds of laughter, conversation, the clinking of glasses... all of it washed over him. Aaron wrapped the noise around his shoulders. He wanted to bury himself in its anonymity.

"That's all you'll be getting from me for the rest of the evening." Alex, the bar owner, folded his hands over his chest. "You've already had five drinks in less than an hour."

A record, even for someone who'd decided to make the bar his second home in the past few months.

But it was not enough.

Not when Aaron could still hear the screams of his twin, Zayn, as that bastard Noah had sliced the sword through him. Noah. An immortal warrior, a fellow Ascendant, had gutted his twin three months ago.

In doing so, he'd torn out the other half of Aaron's soul.

Zayn was gone. In his place, all that remained was a black hole. A darkness that had grown since the moment Zayn's light had blinked out on the psychic web shared by the Ascendants.

With every passing day, his grief expanded, until it twisted his insides. Until he'd become a creature he couldn't recognize anymore. A twinless twin.

Just thinking about it pulsed keening grief through Aaron.

Moving aside the ambrosia, he reached for the bottle with the amber-colored liquid he craved. It was the only thing that helped numb his emotions, blotting out any sign of who he was. Aaron Garcia. The youngest of their group of immortal warriors, since the death of his brother.

Before Alex could protest, Aaron tilted the glass back, letting the liquid burn down his throat. It hit his stomach with a sickening thud that did little to douse the emotions warring there.

Then, just as he'd intended, a veil of blankness crashed between him and the ever-present grief that threatened to overwhelm.

Aaron still felt the pain, but it was a little duller. Only a burning twist of a knife's blade that carved out his heart, leaving him numb.

The harsh sound of Zayn's breathing as he lay dying was muted. He would never forget the feeling of his twin's life seeping out.

It should have been him, the cynical older brother, who had died. Not Zayn. Not the one who'd had so much life. Every time he'd stepped into a room, he'd lit it up. No one who'd met Zayn had remained unaffected by his pure joy of life.

Zayn's vibrancy had provided that much-needed link to everything that was bright.

With his death, Aaron had no anchor.

He reached for his glass, only to miss it. The glass toppled over and hit the floor, smashing to pieces.

Without a pause, Aaron grabbed the almost-empty bottle, raising it to his mouth.

Alex tore it out of his hand. "Enough!" He didn't approve of Aaron trying to drink away his grief.

Neither did his fellow immortal warriors.

Tired of being told off, Aaron had moved out of his barracks in the mayor's complex and into a room just above the bar.

Alex hadn't turned Aaron away. Probably because it was easier for Alex to keep an eye on him that way.

Not that it mattered, as long as Alex kept his tab running and kept the liquor coming every night.

The alcohol had done its job. Aaron didn't feel anything. Not even his legs as he got to his feet… and almost collapsed. Reaching out, Aaron grabbed the bar counter, as if it were his only support in a world gone wrong.

Someone touched his shoulder. The scent of vanilla and sunshine laced with something hot and spicy tugged at his senses.

"You okay, Guardian?"

Aaron turned, and the world tilted.

Golden sparks in green eyes pierced the fog in his head.

She raised her chin. The dark cloud of auburn hair around her face kissed the honey-brown skin of her neck.

The amber pendant nestled in the dip between her delicate collarbones caught the light from above, throwing her face in relief. Cheekbones slanted down to meet a heart-shaped chin.

She was sensuous, yet had just a hint of obstinacy in those eyes to make her intriguing. Those luscious, unpainted lips. He wanted to sink his teeth into them.

Aaron had wanted to shut out the world since Zayn's death. He hadn't thought that when he decided to face reality, it would be like this.

Months of holding back all emotions shattered, and the feelings he'd tried to smother for so long rushed to the forefront.

"Guardian?" That husky voice called him back to the present.

She was addressing him. His black pants and the shirt with the armband were a dead giveaway that he was part of the mayor's elite team of Guardians of the City.

His senses reached out to her. A flare of silver zinged between them on the psychic plane before disappearing so fast he was sure he'd imagined it.

Heat slammed into his chest, and the breath whistled out of him. "Who are you?" He reached up to rub the spot over his chest where it throbbed.

## Hope

He looked at her, and his pain sliced through her as if it were her own.

Those cobalt-blue eyes drew her in, inviting her to drown in them. It was as if he saw straight to her soul, to who she was.

If she let him, he'd strip away her barriers.

His unleashed dominance thrummed against her nerve endings, and Hope's will dissolved.

She wanted to reach out and pour herself into him, to push away the grief that dragged down his spirit.

"Hope?"

Little sparks of awareness skittered over her skin.

He chuckled.

The sound tugged at her lower belly, reaching parts of her they had no business reaching.

"I've been looking for hope."

"Oh?"

The man nodded, eyes intent, framed by long hair that flowed down his back. Cheekbones jutted out, sloping down toward an unruly beard that clung to his features.

Hope wasn't partial to beards, but the look suited him. He felt untamed, wild… and so sexy.

Her dragon shifted, restless, jolting a pulse of heat through her.

One side of his lips twisted, in a smile or a sneer, she couldn't tell. He looked like someone who was trying to hold on to his control. Or someone who was trying his best to not fall over.

He was drunk.

Even in his inebriated state, those glazed eyes held an edge of threat. His T-shirt molded itself to his chest, outlining rippling muscles that marked him as a warrior. Tattoos ran up the side of his right arm, disappearing into the sleeve. He looked lethal.

Yeah, this man had a mind of his own.

Reaching out a finger, he brushed her cheek.

Sizzle.

A jolt of electricity coursed through her. His touch arrowed straight to her core.

On the psychic plane, her dragon lunged for him, anxious to get close, to wrap her wings around this man and inhale his essence. Her dragon recognized this male. Wanted to bond with him.

She reined in her beast.

If she let things progress, they'd sleep together, and Hope knew it would be not be casual. The Guardian's life was in danger. From her.

Her dragon felt connected to Aaron somehow.

It would only make the parting—and they'd have to part—that much more difficult, for both woman and dragon.

Best to stop it before it started.

Besides, she didn't want to hurt him.

She didn't know this man, so why was she so affected by him? Enough to care about his emotional well-being. It didn't make sense at all.

She pulled back, her action so sudden she bumped into the person behind her.

"There, there, darlin'." Hands gripped her waist, straightening her.

Hope turned and looked up, and up. The man was so tall he could only be a shifter.

He grinned down at her. The smell of alcohol from this one was so strong she could have lit his fumes on fire.

There was a growl.

The Guardian slid his body between her and the other drunken male.

His warm and very masculine arm snaked around her waist, holding her flush against his back.

Awesome. Typical male domination.

The two were getting ready to go head to head in a bar. Not quite conducive to the low profile she'd been trying to keep.

The scent of eucalyptus and pine surrounded her. It was as if she were transported to an open hillside. A wildness to the smell sank deep into her soul. It called to that untamed part of her. The one that had her breaking rules to come to this city.

Faced with a back so broad it blocked off the rest of the bar from sight, she watched the muscles bunching under his shirt. She flattened her palm against those muscles, and they shifted under her touch.

"Get your hands off her, Cain," the Guardian growled at the shifter male.

His voice rumbled, setting off tiny vibrations over her skin.

Hope peeked around in time to see Cain fold his arms over his chest.

He was as tall as her Guardian and broader. The shifter was an absolute tank of a man.

"Says who?"

Anger was clearly a sobering emotion. Both males stood tall, chests thrust forward, ready to beat the hell out of each other.

"Says me."

Hope came around to stand at right angles to both.

Slapping a hand on each of their chests, she shoved. Muscles straining with the effort, she managed to hold both of them back.

Each man was bigger than her, yet she'd stopped them. She'd given away how powerful she was even in human form.

Hope darted her attention from one man to the other. Their gazes were fixed on each other, fists curled by their sides.

Her breath whistled out in relief.

They were too engrossed in their macho game of out doing each other.

Amber eyes glowing bright, Cain's gaze dropped to her. He canted his head, nostrils flaring.

He must have caught her scent. He knew she was not human, that she was a shifter.

Stepping back enough that he was out of her reach, Cain raised his hands. "Sorry, bro." He grinned at the other man.

Huh? He was backing off?

Cain clapped the Guardian on his shoulder.

Right, so they knew each other.

"Good to see you looking more like yourself, Aaron."

Aaron. So that was his name. Both the dragon and the woman inside her jumped at that small intimate piece of knowledge.

The Guardian grunted. His muscles vibrated with tension, reminding Hope her palm was still flat against his chest. His very male ripped chest.

She let her palm stay there a second longer before letting it drop to her side.

"What are you doing here? Did the Council send you to keep an eye on me?" Aaron thrust his jaw forward.

"Why would they do that, hmm?" Cain grinned, transforming him into a charismatic male.

No female stood a chance.

Good thing she wasn't attracted to him.

Her head was too full of the other complex, brooding man whose gaze was focused on her face. She had her hands full with the Guardian.

Cain widened his stance, lips twisting in a smirk. "You are more than capable of defending yourself, immortal warrior and Ascendant that you are."

Her gaze swiveled back to Aaron.

Immortal warrior? Ascendant?

Not only had she almost given away what she was, but she had also made contact with the Council of the City. Everything her leader had forbidden her to do.

"Besides," Cain flicked his gaze to Hope, a wicked glint in his eyes, "I think that you've found someone to take care of. You're going to have your hands full. Heed my words, bro, she's not as innocent as she seems."

"Hold on!" Who was this shifter? And why was he presuming any connection between her and the Guardian? "I'm still here, you know." She waved her hands in front of his face.

Cain just smirked, blinking slowly.

"You were never drunk, were you?" She realized in a flash of insight: "It was all an act to get a rise out of your friend."

"He damned well succeeded."

Her attention darted back to Aaron's face.

Those cobalt-blue eyes narrowed.

Why was he was so angry? "You're jealous? Because your friend touched me?" Hope looked back, only to see that Cain—the traitor—had melted into the crowd.

That left her with one irate immortal who had the ability to twist her insides, with an emotion she didn't quite want to name.

When she turned back to Aaron, his eyes were clearer. Perhaps he was beginning to see just how illogical his actions were?

Swooping down, he brushed his lips across hers.

Okay. Perhaps not.

*To find out what happens next, get* Inception *here*

Get all Laxmi's books here

**Knotted Omega Series**
**Dark Dystopian Romance**

Wanted by the Alpha
Taken by the Alpha
Claimed by the Alpha
Owned by the Alpha

**Fae's Claim**
**Dark Paranormal Romance Series**

Stolen by the Fae
Property of the Fae
Taken by the Fae

**Dragon Protectors Series**

**Dragon Protectors Boxed Set (8 books + exclusive prologues and epilogues)**

**Inception** (Hope and Aaron)
**Obsession** (Eve and Cain)
**Deception** (Pandora and Rage)
**Forbidden** (Freya and Axel)
**Seduction** (Neo and Trinity)
**Ascension** (Mira and Zach)
**Revelation** (Arjun and Naya)
**Temptation** (Vance and Serena)

## Many Lives
### Paranormal romance
### (Prequel to Dragon Protectors)

**Awakened** (Ruby and Vik)
**Feral (**Maya and Luke)
**Taken (**Jai and Ariana)
**Redemption** (Mikhail and Leana)
**Claimed** (Kris and Tara)
**Many Lives Box Set** (6 books including Fated, with FREE bonus scenes, prologues and epilogues)

## Many Lives Origin Stories

**Origin**
**Chosen**

## Contemporary Romance

**Love, Caution (Jace) - Bad Boy Billionaire Romance**

# FREE BOOKS

*CONNECT ON MESSENGER TO CLAIM YOUR FREE BOOKS BEFORE I CHANGE MY MIND*

# ABOUT THE AUTHOR

Laxmi is a New York Times Bestselling Author who writes paranormal and contemporary romance. Her pen name Scarlette Brooke writes dark romance with a twist.

Happily married, she lives in London and PS she insists that you call her Lax :)

CONNECT ON MESSENGER TO CLAIM YOUR FREE BOOK HERE

FOLLOW ON AMAZON HERE

FOLLOW ON BOOKBUB HERE

ON GOODREADS

JOIN HER READER GROUP FOR EXCLUSIVE SNEAK PEEKS

❧ Created with Vellum

Printed in Great Britain
by Amazon